DEDI

*For my sister, Lynne-Maree, who taught me to always fight for what we want in life and to never stop reaching for our dreams.*

*Fused*
*"to come together to form a single unit"*

# PROLOGUE

*G*UILTY. The word repeats through my mind as the sound of the judge's gavel bangs heavily, echoing in the courtroom. I can't believe what I'm hearing. *Guilty.* The word keeps repeating. I know the judge is delivering the sentence, but I can't concentrate on anything other than that one word.

I look across to my sister, Holly, my twin, my other half, and see the tears free falling down her face—her hands are trembling slightly. Holly brings her eyes to meet mine. No words are needed. I know exactly what is going through her head right now. What the fuck are we going to do now? How do we survive this?

Holly is sitting on the other side of my mother, both of us grasping one of her hands in ours, knowing if we let go, even for a minute, she would crumble to the floor. My mother's tears are not silent. Her cries I'm sure can be heard across the city.

As I sit here, repeating the word over and over in my head, I have to wonder how much one woman can take before she completely breaks. My mother is strong, probably one of the strongest women I know, but this last year, to say it's been tough is an understatement.

My little brother Dylan was killed in a car accident. My mum was driving home after a footy game when a drunk driver swerved into her lane. She escaped with a broken leg, my brother, my baby brother who was only fifteen, died on impact. Making the sign of the cross, I send a little prayer upwards as I think of my brother. I've never been a very religious person; each prayer I've sent heavenly these past twelve months has gone unanswered and a bit of my faith has diminished alongside them.

There was a court case for the drunk driver, where he got off. He killed my brother and managed to get out of doing any time in a cell, where he bloody belonged. This destroyed my father, to know that the person who killed his son was out walking around free. It did not sit well with him.

My father decided to take matters into his own hands. He followed the drunk home one day and shot him, point blank in the head. A clear kill shot. I don't feel any remorse for the drunk, maybe I should. Maybe I'm a horrible person not caring that my dad took the life of another. But that son of a bitch killed my brother and has led to the events of today. To my family being torn apart even more.

At seventeen years old, I've just finished high school and should be out celebrating and living life to the fullest before I have to start university next year. But as I hold my mother's weeping body up, and attempt to listen as the judge drones on, all I can think is how am I going to survive this? How are my mum and sister going to survive this?

My father has just been sentenced for murder. He's been my rock my whole life, and now I have to figure out how to get by without him, without having his support and guidance, his unyielding love.

My mother's scream startles me out of my thoughts and I watch as she falls to the floor, Holly dragged down with her force. I can see her heart breaking. They were supposed to grow old together. My mum and dad were the definition of soulmates, of true love.

As I watch my mother crumble, I make a promise there and then that I will never let a man have that kind of hold over me. I will never get so attached to a man that my life would fall apart the moment they are no longer in it. And I swear on everything holy that I will never let myself fall in love.

# CHAPTER ONE

*Reilly*

*I* FEEL like I'm in a furnace. *Why is it so damn hot in here?* Wait, where is here? As the sleep fog slowly recedes from my brain, and the more alert I become, the more the realisation that I'm not in my own bed sinks in.

My stealthy attempt to roll out from beneath the heavy arm currently draped over my waist is stopped when that arm grips me tighter, pulling my back right up against a chest. I freeze, hoping not to wake whoever that arm belongs to.

Taking a look down at that arm, that very muscular and tattooed arm, a not so silent moan escapes my lips. The events of last night slowly returning to my mind, I know just who that arm belongs to. And the body that goes with that arm, comes in the form of a six-foot something with muscle on top of muscle. Just thinking of what that body can, and did, do to mine has me re-thinking my escape plan.

What can one more round in the hay hurt? One more glorious moment of our bodies fusing together before I make my break and never indulge in this body of sin again. I squirm, rubbing my ass into his crotch. I can feel his hardness as I continue to squirm against him.

The arm around me tightens, somehow pulling my body even tighter against his. His gravelly voice murmurs in my ear, causing goosebumps to rise all over my body.

"You know, babe, if you want junior to come out to play, all you have to do is ask? He'd be willing to be yours anytime."

Rolling over to face him, I grab his junior in my hand and stroke it up and down slowly.

"*Mmm*, I think I'd like to have a playdate with junior just one more time before I have to go," I declare, ducking my head down, not able to make eye contact with him.

I don't know why but the man makes me freaking nervous. He causes butterflies, no, not butterflies, more like a hive of bees buzzing around my stomach. It's unnerving, and usually I'd be out the door before he could blink. But his junior, I know what that thing can do, and I want more of it. *Just one more time*, I tell myself.

"Babe, if you think I'm letting you go after just one more time, think again." His voice is so stern and serious, I look up into eyes that are trained onto my face. Shit, I think he might actually be serious. Just as I'm about to refute his claims that he can keep me, I'm interrupted by the banging of a door. But it's what's yelled through the house that has my body freezing and my mind in a panic.

"Police, open up!"

More banging ensues and more demands to open up. Bray curses under his breath as he jumps out of bed and makes quick work of putting clothes on. Looking back at me, he says, "Whatever you do, stay here. Do not leave this room. I want you here in this bed when I sort this shit out."

Well, fuck that. I'm pulled from my dazed and lust-filled brain and chuck on the first thing I find discarded on the floor. Which happens to be the shirt he was wearing last night.

My eyes scan the bedroom and land on my phone. Picking it up, I head for the door. Just as my hand lands on the handle, Bray's hand closes around mine, stopping my hasty escape.

"Reilly, you've lost your damn mind if you think for a minute, I'm letting you walk out of here, especially dressed like that."

Pulling my hand out from under his, I turn and shove at his chest, his rock-hard freaking chest. Instead of letting my thoughts wander to what I could do with that chest, I let the anger boil up inside of me, the frustration that I put myself into this position. I can still remember when those knocks and those words were said through the door of my childhood home, only they weren't looking for some guy I just met. No, they were looking for my father.

I can feel the tears threaten to escape my eyes with the memories, which only makes me madder. I am not this vulnerable. I do not let myself be this vulnerable girl. I'm strong, independent, and I plan to keep it that way.

I push him further away from me, which he obviously allows me to do because, let's face it, there's no way I could actually move this hulk of a man. "No, you don't get to tell me what I can and can't do. You and I, we had a great time last night, but that's it. I'm out. I hope you enjoy your time in handcuffs," I say as I step back to the door.

Bray goes to take a step towards me and I hold my hand out to stop him. "If you so much as touch me right now, or try to stop me from leaving this room, I will scream bloody murder, and those cops out there will break your door down, I'm sure."

I watch as he takes a step back, his fists clenching and unclenching as he watches me walk out the door. I can feel him behind me the whole way through the house. I don't turn back to look though.

Pulling the door wide open, I give the officers my brightest smile. "Officers, I believe the man you're looking for is right behind me. You all have a nice day now."

Walking down the path, I don't stop, I don't look back, and I don't let the first tear fall until I'm halfway down the street and out of view.

Swiping the traitorous tears from my face, I straighten my shoulders. I will not let myself go back to that place, back to the memories of my dad being taken away in cuffs. Shit, I have no idea where the hell I even am. How am I going to get home?

"Okay, you can do this, Reilly, just call Holly. She will come and get you." I know I probably look like an escapee from the mental asylum right now. I'm currently wearing a man's t-shirt and nothing else; although said shirt falls down just above my knees. It doesn't matter that I'm more covered than I was last night in the club, yet somehow, I feel so much more exposed. The fact that I'm talking to myself does not make me seem any saner right now.

I call Holly, who, after screeching her way through her holier than thou lecture about yet again having to collect my ass from a strange neighbourhood, agrees to come and pick me up.

So now I'm sitting under a huge shady gum tree, waiting. As I take in my surroundings of a tree-lined street with huge mansions, I'm in awe as well as shock that this is the street Bray lives on. It is not what I would have picked for him. This street screams the family home, wife, husband, 2.5 kids and a dog. Not the hot as sin, tatted-up bad boy I had last night.

*I squeal as I'm swiftly thrown over a shoulder, a big broad shoulder. Clinging to the back of his shirt, I can feel the muscles clenching underneath as he carries me through his house. My head upside down, I can't even get a good look at his home as he makes his way through to what I'm hoping is his bedroom.*

*"Bray, let me down. I can walk. I'm too heavy and you'll probably put your back out or something, and I really like this back. I wouldn't want to hurt it."*

*"Not a chance in hell am I putting you down, pumpkin. Well, not until I'm throwing you down onto my bed, which is happening real soon." He slaps my ass before he adds, "Don't ever fucking try to tell me that you're too heavy again. Your body is the definition of perfection."*

*Mmm, I can't help but squirm at the stinging pain on my ass. As hard as I try not to let the moan escape my mouth, it does. Bray takes note of my reaction, groaning and landing another, firmer slap to my butt.*

*"Like it a little rough, huh? Good news for you, babe, I like to fuck rough and hard. Get ready, because you're in for a night you won't be forgetting anytime soon."*

*All of a sudden, I'm flying through the air, landing on my back, on what can only be described as a cloud. Damn, is this his bed? I don't think I've ever felt anything so bloody soft and comfy. I don't have time to contemplate the quality of Bray's mattress and bedding; my mind is imme-diately drawn to the hulk of a man currently pulling his* shirt over the back of his head, revealing one hell of a body.

My eyes travel from his broad shoulders and wide chest down to his—wait, is that an eight pack? My attempts at counting are

interrupted by his commanding voice, snapping me out of my daze.

"Strip, now, Reilly. I won't ask again."

Staring up at him, I'm both at a loss for words and confused at the wetness that just pooled between my legs by his demand. Or is that from the sight in front of me? Because let me tell you, the sight of a shirtless Brayden Williamson is enough to have any girl weeping.

The next thing that registers with my brain is the sound of material ripping. Holy shit, I look down to see my dress literally ripped in half. What the hell? Lifting my eyes to meet Bray's, I momentarily get lost in those emerald beauties.

"What the fuck, Bray? That was one of my favourite dresses!" "I told you to strip. You were too slow." He lifts an eyebrow at me, just begging for me to argue.

"Well, maybe give a girl some bloody warning next time you plan to just strip your shirt off. I can't help it if I was momentarily lost in the Bray-effect. You're replacing this dress, and just so you know, it wasn't cheap."

Bray leans down, capturing my lips in his and not so gently parting them to invade my mouth with his tongue. The argument is literally sucked out of me as he kisses the ever-loving shit out of me. Man, I thought I'd been kissed before. But this... this kiss is the one they write movies about.

*Grabbing the back of his neck, I pull him closer to me, holding as tight as I can.*

*Breaking the kiss, Bray trails his tongue down my neck, kissing, nibbling and biting his way down to my breast. With a groan, he grasps both breasts in his hands before taking my right nipple into his mouth. My body arching off the bed at the contact, I shiver as shots of pleasure shoot straight to my core.*

*It's not long before he's pulling my panties down my legs. I barely register that he's moving before he has my legs spread wide open with his head buried between them. Oh, God, looking down at him was a mistake. The hungry look in his eyes as he licks his lips is almost enough to send my quivering mess of a body over the edge.*

*"Tell me, pumpkin, do you taste as sweet as you look? Because this has to be, hands down, the prettiest goddamn pussy I've ever seen." He growls as he bites into my inner thigh.*

*"Oh, God... Oh, God!" My hips are bucking all on their own, in an attempt to get the friction to my core that it so desperately seeks.*

*"No, I believe, 'oh, Bray' are the words you want to be screaming, babe," Bray states just a moment before he dives his tongue into my centre, licking me from bottom to top. "Mmm, damn, pumpkin, this pussy is dangerous. One lick and I think I'm addicted." Bray makes quick work of diving back in.*

*Moments later, I'm screaming his name as the orgasm of the century rolls through me. Every nerve ending in my body is on fire, exploding with sensation. What the hell is he doing to me?*

*I must have blacked out for a minute because when I open my eyes, Bray is standing in front of the bed. Naked. Completely fucking naked. Thank you to any God who created this masterpiece. My eyes travel hungrily over his body, down his torso eagerly, wanting a glimpse at... wait a hot darn minute. Is that... oh my God, it is.*

*My mouth waters at the sight of his cock, his pierced, beautiful, huge fucking cock. I lick my lips. I can't wait to get a taste of that. Did I mention pierced? Yep, pierced. A Prince Albert, shiny metal sitting on the head of his cock.*

*Beep! Beep!* "Reilly, get up! Come on, I don't have all day!" I'm immediately drawn out of my daydream or memory, whatever you want to call it, by the sound of my sister's voice screaming at me.

Get it together, Reilly. I try my mental pep talk. I'm feeling like a bitch in heat right now. Just the memory of Bray's cock has me wanting to beg for more of it. No, I can't go there. I will not go there.

Getting up off the ground, I'm further reminded of what magic that pierced cock is capable of as my core both burns and tingles with the remnants of last night's events.

I do everything I can to avoid making eye contact with Holly on the drive home. If I look over at her, she will know the internal struggle I'm doing my darndest to fight off. Just as I thought Holly was actually going to let me sit here in peace for the whole ride home, she decided to break the silence. Reaching over, she picked up my hand and threaded her fingers with mine.

"Okay, enough wallowing. What happened?" she questions while giving my hand a squeeze before letting it go.

Turning my head to give her my best glare, I respond, "I'm not wallowing, nothing happened. I was up late and I'm tired, that's all."

"Nice try, Rye, but I'm not buying it." She shakes her head no, using her teacher voice on me. I hate to admit, it is actually a little scary and firm, almost makes me want to confess everything so I'm not in trouble.

Looking over at Holly, I already know there's no point trying to hide anything from her. We have never been able to hide anything from each other. It's some sort of weird twin thing; we always just know whatever the other is feeling.

As much as I want to confide in her, I just don't think I can right now. She would try to understand, but really, she's never been in this situation. She's never even had a one-night stand. Holly is the relationship or nothing kind of girl. She's looking for her prince charming to share the white picket fence with and 2.5 kids. Meanwhile, I made a promise to myself a long time ago that I would never let myself get attached to a guy.

Holly has always been the good twin, while I prefer to blur the lines and break the rules. Her personality is the complete opposite of mine. She's a kindergarten teacher, loves the kid's she teaches like they were her own, and cries her eyes out at the end of each year when they move up a grade to a new teacher.

Although our personalities may be opposite, our looks are identical. Only those who really know us are able to tell us apart from each other. We share the same tall, thin stature, long red hair with pale skin and green eyes. The only difference being Holly has a tiny freckle under her left eye.

My silence does not get her to back down at all. "Rye, you know I love you most in the world. Please tell me what the hell happened, or I might just turn this car around and hunt down Bray. I'm not afraid to get my hands dirty if I need to, you know. I will emasculate him if he hurt you." Her voice is getting louder. I know she really would turn the car around too.

"You would have a hard time getting to him, Holl, considering the cops banged down his door and arrested him. Hence, why I had to call you to come and get me at this ungodly hour."

Holly looks over at me with sympathy written all over her face. "Rye, I'm sorry. What was he arrested for?"

"I don't know. I chucked on a shirt..." Looking down at said shirt, I then add, "His shirt, grabbed my phone and got the hell out of dodge. I didn't stick around to have a cuppa with the officers, Holly. And frankly, I don't give a shit what he was arrested for. It's his problem not mine."

As I finish my rant, it hits me. I'm wearing his damn shirt, no wonder I can't get him and his magical cucumber out of my bloody head. I can smell him. It's an exotic, earthy scent. It's an odd feeling; I'm torn between being repulsed, because that's how I should be feeling, and a sense of comfort and security in being able to smell him. Okay, it's official. I've gone and lost my damn mind.

As we're pulling into the driveway, Holly locks the car door, stopping my plan of a quick escape.

"Reilly, you know whatever it is, it could have just been a misunderstanding. Not everyone who gets arrested ends up in jail. You like him, I can tell. You like him more than you want to. You should just ask him." With that, Holly unlocks the door, leaving me sitting there contemplating her words.

Before getting in the shower and before I can think better of it, I call Alyssa to let her know that Bray was dragged off in handcuffs. Let's just say the conversation was short-lived with me ending it promptly when she started to question how I knew Bray was dragged off in handcuffs. *Arghh,* I shouldn't have called her, of course he would have called his brother for help already. And really, why the hell do I care if he's left rotting in a cell alone or not? I don't, at least that's what I'm telling myself anyway.

I've just had one of the longest showers of my life. Boy, did my body need the hot water streaming down on it. I feel like I've ran a marathon; my muscles are sore in places I didn't know even existed. Not to mention the fact that every time I sit down, I can still feel—nope, not going there again.

As I make my way back to my bedroom, my phone is vibrating on the bedside table where I left it charging. Unplugging the phone, I scroll through what seems to be a million notifications of text messages. Most from an unknown number, a lot from an unknown number. But there is also one from Alyssa.

The curiosity of the unknown number wins out, so I check those first.

**UNKNOWN**: *Where are you?*

**UNKNOWN**: *Hello? I'm giving you thirty minutes, babe. If I don't hear from you, I will come looking.*

. . .

**UNKNOWN**: *I'm serious. I will hunt you down if I have to!*

**UNKNOWN**: *Reilly, please just tell me you at least made it home safely.*

**UNKNOWN**: *Twenty minutes left, pumpkin.*

**UNKNOWN**: *Fifteen minutes, tell me where you are.*

OKAY, obviously these are from Bray, but if he thinks I'm texting him back, he can think again. I don't even know how he got my number. Without overthinking it, I save his number to my phone before moving onto Alyssa's messages.

**ALYSSA**: *Reilly, how much do you love me? Actually, don't answer that. It doesn't matter because the amount is about to grow tenfold!!*

**ALYSSA**: *I hope you're sitting down. Are you ready? Okay, here it is. I, yes, me, Alyssa, just landed you your dream PR job at only the hottest nightclub in town. The*

*Merge, ever heard of it? Lol. Anyway, Zac fired his PR lady #bitch last night and I suggested he interview you. He skipped the interview and is giving you a trial; you need to be at the club in two hours.*

OH MY GOD! *Ahh!* Jumping around and doing a happy dance, I pull myself together enough to text Alyssa back. I cannot believe I have a job at The Merge. It's like winning the damn lottery. I'm starting to like this Zac more and more.

**ME:** *Alyssa, OMG! I freaking love you, girl!!! Thank you! Boy, you must have really screwed that poor boy's brains out last night for him to just give me a job like that. Anyway, whatever you did to that cucumber, keep doing it! Tell him I'll be there.*

**ALYSSA:** *Don't worry, I plan on keeping this cucumber around. I think I really like this one, Rye. And don't think you're off the hook. I know something went on with you and Bray last night. I want deets.*

**ME:** *Sorry, gotta go get ready. I have a job to get to.*

. . .

JUST AS I'M walking into my closet, my phone beeps again. Looking down at the screen, my smile falters, as I see the notification from JTPC, the abbreviated version of my warning to myself, that this one I need to stay clear of. Junior the pierced cucumber. No, Reilly, you are not letting him ruin this happy moment for you. I can't help myself; I open the message up.

JTPC: *Reilly, I know you're on your phone right now. I can see your messages with Alyssa. Answer me, please. I just need to know that you made it home.*

BEFORE I HAVE the chance to message him back, telling him where he can shove his concern, another message comes through.

JTPC: *Look, I know it was not an ideal situation this morning, but it's been sorted out. I'm sorry you had to wake up to that. Please, for the love of God, tell me you're at home and that you're okay.*

NOT IDEAL, that's laughable. Having the cops banging on the door to arrest the guy you just did all sorts of compromising things with the night before is so far from bloody ideal. My blood is now boiling. I'm mad and I am going to let him have it.

**ME:** *Not Ideal??? You have to be bloody joking, right? You were ARRESTED, Bray. There is nothing ideal about having the cops bang down the door of the guy you were banging the night before! Asshole. Don't message me anymore. I'm fine. Last night was fun and all, but let's leave it at that.*

SWITCHING MY PHONE ONTO SILENT, I throw it over

to my bed and hunt for the perfect first day on the job outfit.

# CHAPTER TWO

*Bray*

AFTER SITTING in the police station for two fucking hours, the last thing I want to do is ride along while my brother plays fucking Uber for his girlfriend. But, as always, whenever my ass has needed bailing out of anything, Zac has always been there, always willing to fight for me.

Ever since our parents died five years ago, Zac has been there; he stepped up, taking guardianship of Ella and me. Let's just say, in no way did I make it easy for him. I was seventeen when my parents were mugged at a train station, my mother falling onto the tracks as the mugger snatched her bag from her shoulder. My father jumped down to help her, but they couldn't get back onto the platform in time.

Zac can't talk about the incident; Ella still cries

when she thinks no one is watching or noticing. Me, I just got angry, really fucking angry. I would pick fights with anyone. I was eventually kicked out of school because of it. Fighting helped me though. I needed the pain, the adrenaline, somewhere to focus all of my fucking rage on so it wouldn't consume me.

I joined up in an underground street fighting club—I was good. But it didn't take long for Zac to pull me out. He signed me up for a state-of-the-art MMA gym. Got me in with a great coach and the rest is history. I still fight underground, still have that same great fucking coach. The only difference is now I fight for our own underground club.

Once Zac realised fighting was part of me and what I needed to do, he once again took control and built an underground cage in the basement of his nightclub, The Merge. The Merge Cage is now known as the best in town, our fights get packed audiences, and hundreds of thousands of dollars are bet at our fights. Even more when it's my cage name, Braydon Johnson, on the card.

I'm fucking good at what I do, undefeated, and I will take on any motherfucker who wants to try to beat my ass. The advantage I have? I still have the pool of rage I've carried around with me since I was seventeen; the one place I let myself release that rage is in the cage.

My thoughts are halted as Zac's girlfriend, Alyssa, opens her door in a fucking towel. Damn, I know she's my brother's girl, but fuck, she is hot as hell. Although I can appreciate her hotness, that's where it ends; there is no spark, no chemistry. But there is some kind of weird pull to this girl I can't seem to wrap my mind around. It's like I want to protect her; from what, I don't know.

Maybe it's just that this is the first girl who Zac has actually given two fucks about, and she's good for him. It's early days, but I can see that she's not going anywhere; this one is sticking. That doesn't mean I can't have some fun and piss my brother off a little in the process though. After all, what are little brother's for, if not for being annoying little shits.

Peering around Zac's side, I tease, "Damn, I can see why my brother has given up his balls to you, Lyssa." I raise my eyebrows up and down suggestively.

It doesn't take long for Zac to step inside, blocking my view of Alyssa and slamming the door in my face.

"I'll just wait in the car, kids!" I yell out to the door. Heading back to the car, I lean against it and pull out my phone.

Ever since Reilly stormed out of my fucking house, I haven't been able to get her off my mind. I need to know where the hell she is. Did she get home safely? Fuck's sake, I sound like my fucking brother now.

Rubbing a hand across my chin, I think about whether or not I should text, call or, fuck, just track her down and rock up on her doorstep. Maybe with a bow wrapped around junior, one that she can unwrap with

24

her mouth. Straight away junior stands to attention, on board with the idea as much as I am.

Looking down, I say, "Settle down, mate. It's not gonna happen for us right this second." I'm out here standing in a carpark talking to my fucking cock. Yep, fuck my life.

Deciding that texting is probably the safest bet for both junior and me, considering the state of anger Reilly left in, I pull up her number; the one I had to steal from her phone while she was sleeping, mind you.

When I asked her for her number last night in the club, she laughed right in my fucking face and replied with, "Yeah, that's never going to happen, stud muffin, but what could happen is you getting me a refill." She then proceeded to shove her glass into my chest before reaching up onto her tippy-toes and whispering in my ear, "And, at the end of the night, you can take me home to bed for one hell of a night you won't be forgetting anytime soon."

Needless to say, I did get her that refill. My eyes never strayed far from her for the rest of the night. Which is also the reason that the fucker who hit Alyssa across the face was able to get so close to her. The rage that overtook my body, mind and soul at seeing some fucker hit Alyssa was off the charts. I barely know the girl, yet I have this weird need to protect her. The same way I want to protect Ella from the whole damn world.

I jumped straight into action without any thought other than killing the guy there and then. My vision went red, zoned in on my target and when I got him, a right hook had him on the ground. But did I stop there? No, I jumped on him, landing punch after punch to his face, then his ribs. The cocksucker didn't stand a chance, and if it wasn't for Dean pulling me back, I would have fucking ended him. Who the fuck hits a bloody woman? A lowlife, that's who. One that should be wiped off the face of the earth and I'm more than happy to be the one to do it.

It's the same fucking cocksucker who thought he could press charges against me, not that those charges stuck. As soon as Zac showed up at the cop shop—with Dean in tow and video footage of the guy hitting Alyssa, which, mind you, up until that point Zac had not seen—I was released. When Zac did see that footage, he lost it and picked up a chair, throwing it across the room and smashing the mirrored window. Needless to say, the cops dropped the charges. But even without that footage, Zac would have just pulled some strings higher up in the department.

Shaking off the thoughts of last night and this morning, I fire off a text to Reilly, asking her where she is. Waiting for her to reply, I think I check my phone a dozen times before Alyssa comes bouncing out by herself, wearing fucking nurses' scrubs. Man, maybe I need to visit the hospital more often if this is how nurses are looking these days.

Thinking she's just going to make her way over to the car and wait for Zac, I'm taken by surprise when she comes up to me, wrapping her arms around my neck and hugging the shit out of me.

Damn, this girl can hug. It's a bloody good thing junior took my advice and settled down, or she'd be getting more out of this hug than she bargained for. I wrap my arms around her, returning the hug.

"Thank you for helping me last night, Bray. It really means a lot to me that you would stick up for me like that," she whispers in my ear.

"Anytime, sister," I say back to her while smirking over her shoulder at Zac, who is now glaring and storming toward us.

"What the fuck?" Zac yells out, while pulling Alyssa behind him and attempting to land a right hook to my face. One that I easily duck and avoid. I know if he really wanted to land that hook, he would have been able to. I just laugh at him as Alyssa wraps her arms around him and calms his ass down. She has an uncanny way of being able to do that to him. I might have to hit her up for some pointers. Although, I suspect it may have something to do with the anatomy between her legs. Which, obviously, junior does not share any similarities with.

"You know it was bound to happen, right? It didn't take her long at all to come to her senses already and decide I'm the hotter brother after all," I tell him.

"Fuck off, idiot," he says while slapping me across the back of my head. No matter how big I get, that's always the move he goes for to reprimand me for my antics. I'd never tell him this, but when he does that, he reminds me a lot of our dad. Sometimes I say stupid shit on purpose just to get that glimpse of my dad, even if for just a second.

SITTING in the back of the car listening to Zac and Alyssa swoon over each other is bloody sickening. I'm half listening as I type out increasingly frustrated texts to Reilly. Why the hell is she not answering me? Where the fuck is she? What if something happened to her when she left my place?

I live in a good neighbourhood, but still, you don't know who is living next door to you, no matter how nice or expensive the house might be. And, damn it, all she was wearing was my fucking t-shirt.

I'm momentarily distracted remembering the sight of her in nothing but my shirt, those long lean legs of hers on display, her fiery red hair a mess down her back. She was definitely sporting the just fucked hair look. The just thoroughly fucked look, if I must say, and yes, I must.

When Alyssa mentions how much she appreciates Zac giving her a ride, I can't help but laugh a little. She turns around in her seat and glares at me. "Care to share why you got arrested this morning and had to drag Zac out of bed to bail you out?"

What the fuck? How the hell does she know about that? Reaching out, I slap Zac across the back of his head.

Yeah, how do you like it, motherfucker? "You told her? What happened to the bro code, man, bros before—"

I don't get to finish the sentence before Zac is once again scolding me.

But what Alyssa admits leaves me with a sickeningly huge smile plastered across my face, one that I can't seem to stop. "He didn't have to tell me. Reilly sent me a message this morning, worried about you and the fact you got taken away in handcuffs," she says while squinting her eyes at me.

If she's waiting for me to confirm that Reilly was there this morning when I got arrested, she will die waiting. I may not be much of a gentleman, but I do not kiss and tell. So, Reilly was worried about me enough to call Alyssa. Hope is not lost after all. Then the question is why the fuck is she not returning my messages?

I try my best to pretend to be busy on my phone.

Informing Alyssa about what got me arrested is on a need- to-know basis, and she does not in fact need to know. Normally it wouldn't be such a secret, but because I was arrested for beating the crap out of the guy who hit her, I can't tell her. I have a feeling she would get all guilty and shit. I do not need her feeling bad. If she feels bad, Zac's going to feel bad and when Zac feels bad, we all fucking cop the brunt of it.

Alyssa must realise I'm not going to comment on Reilly, and she starts threatening my manhood if I hurt one of her friends. I feel like asking what she would do if one of her friends hurts me, because let's face it, that's the more likely scenario here. Not that I have the feels or anything for Reilly, but I sure wouldn't mind feeling her underneath me again, the sooner the fucking better.

When Zac starts talking about the need to hire a new PR manager for The Merge, and Alyssa recommends Reilly for the job, I can't help but say no to the suggestion. Being around that body all day or night will be torture if she does not let me touch her again. Of course, Zac, the fucker, likes to bloody torture me. He tells Alyssa to let Reilly know she has the job on a trial basis.

I have mixed feelings; on one hand, I'll know where she is and I'll be able to see her all the time. On the other hand, my balls. My poor, poor balls; the friends to junior are going to be fucking blue. Just thinking about her body is driving me crazy. How the hell am I going to handle being around her?

I can see over Alyssa's shoulder that she is texting with Reilly, and the fact that she's answering her texts and not mine is pissing me off. It's also putting a fire inside me. You can run, pumpkin, but just try to hide from me—I dare you to.

I send her another text, letting her know I know she's currently holding her phone, and I know she can see my messages. I also figure I should apologise for this morning's events. I'm sure it was not what she expected. Having the cops bang down your door at ungodly hours in the morning is not ideal.

Her reply makes me smile. She's mad and I can picture her face now—I can picture her pale skin turning red. It's probably all kinds of messed up, but the image of her mad is fucking turning me on. Deciding to let her text slide and let her think she's won, I don't text back. I know she's going to be at the club in a few hours and my day just cleared up. I might just have to stop by and help my bro out for a bit.

As soon as I get home, I head for a shower. I need to wash away the stress of the morning—it's not every day you get arrested, especially just days after you disposed of a fucking corpse. It's not how I had planned my morning to go.

No, I planned on having Reilly for breakfast, then having breakfast off Reilly, then feeding Reilly breakfast. I'm sure you get my drift; it was meant to be a damn pleasurable morning. I can recall the taste of her on my tongue—it's fucking divine. I've never wanted to eat a pussy out so much in my life. I could spend my life with my head buried between her legs.

Junior's on board with the plan too, currently straining at the thought. Taking some shower gel in my hand, I slowly stroke my cock, sliding up and down, putting just the right amount of pressure on it and twisting my hand around at the knob—right where my Prince Albert sits. It doesn't take long for me to work up the speed. Thoughts of Reilly's taste, her smell, her moans, the feel of her soft pale skin under my fingers consume me. I groan out loud. *Fuck*. Before I know it, I'm coming all over the damn wall of the shower while calling out her name.

WALKING BACK INTO MY BEDROOM, I instantly smell her. Fucking hell, is there anywhere I can go without her entering my fucking head? Because I'm a sucker for pain, I inhale the scent. I pick up her discarded, ripped dress off the floor. Taking a picture of the tag and dress, I send a text to Ella.

**ME:** *Ella, sweetheart, do me a favour. Find this particular dress somewhere and buy two of them for me, in this same size, please.*

BECAUSE SHE'S eighteen and has her phone glued to her hand twenty-four/seven, her reply is immediate.

**ELLA:** *Why do you want to buy a dress, or two dresses? I don't think that size will even fit over one of your arms, Bray.*

. . .

**ME:** *Because I ruined someone's dress and need to replace it. So please, just do what you're good at and shop. I need these dresses yesterday. Please?*

ADDING a please on the end may just persuade her to do it; this is not a task I want to have to do myself. Where the hell do they sell these anyway?

**ELLA:** *OKAY, do not need to know how you ruined that dress. Just so you know, that brand is expensive. This is not going to be cheap for you. And while I'm swiping your card, I will be putting a little something extra on it for myself. Call it a personal shopper's fee.*

**ME:** *I wasn't about to tell you how. And I don't care what it costs, just get them. Don't go overboard on your shopper's fee. Love you, sissy. You're the best!*

WALKING BACK out to the living room, I notice a sparkling object on the floor. Picking it up, my smile widens as I inspect the little purse thing that Reilly was carrying around last night. Well, looks like someone was in so much of a rush to leave this morning that they forgot to take their purse with them.

Opening it up, I see a range of cards, including her driver's licence, which has her address on it. I snap a picture of it with my phone. I know that I'm bordering on stalker material here, but I don't really give a fuck. She's going to want this purse back, and she's going to have to come and get it. When she does, I might just have to tie her to my bed and show her what she's missing by denying junior and me.

# CHAPTER THREE

*Reilly*

AKING one last look at myself in the mirror before I head over to The Merge where I am, as of today, gainfully employed, I'm pretty happy with what I've managed to pull off in such a short timeframe.

I'm wearing a black pencil skirt that ends just over my knees and has a split that runs half-way up the front of my left leg. I pulled out my favourite go-to, white, sheer blouse. The neckline is high and hugs around the base of my neck, while the sleeves flow loosely down my arms. I've put on a white crop top underneath; you can see just a hint of skin between where the crop top ends and my skirt begins on my waist. The outfit is finished off with a pair of black pumps, adding a little extra height to my already tall frame.

Not having time to do anything with my hair, I settled for tying it up in a ponytail—one just like Holly usually sports. I'm satisfied that I'm pulling off my professional, badass business bitch look, which let's face it, I need to, considering the only side of me that Zac—aka my new boss and my best girl's new boo—has ever seen of me is the drunk, carefree party girl Reilly. I need to prove that I'm also a professional who is damn good at what I do.

Picking up my black Ted Baker Audrey bag, I start looking around for the clutch I had all my cards in last night. Then it dawns on me. "Fucking Bray," I say out loud to the empty room. I know exactly where I left that clutch last night—right on the floor of his living room where it fell out of my hands, due to being upside down over his damn shoulder.

I'll just text him later and get him to pass it onto Alyssa; that way, I won't need to face him. Yes, that's what I'll do.

Making my way out to my car, I smile when I see it, my beast, my baby, my ride, the one ride I don't mind driving over and over again. Turning the key over, I listen as the engine of my black Mustang GT convertible roars to life. I'm not really sure how he did it, but my dad had cars delivered to both Holly and me on our university graduation day. Holly got her dream yellow VW bug, and me, I got this machine.

WALKING up to the back entrance to the club, I approach as the door opens and a wall of muscle clothed in black stands between me and the inside of the club. I have to tilt my head back to meet the wall's face. I reach his face as his eyes not so subtly rake up and down my body. Clearing my throat, I gain his attention.

"Are you lost?" the wall asks with a raised eyebrow.

Tilting my head, I squint my eyes at him. I'm about to get *riled Reilly* on his ass when I remember that this is now my place of business. Taking a deep breath, I gather myself before I respond to him. Holding my hand out, I say, "No, I'm Reilly. Zac's expecting me."

"Yeah, that's what they all say. Sorry, love, but Zac's not interested." The wall steps back, planning to shut the door in my face. I react without thinking and stick my foot out to catch the door, only to have the door slam into the inside of my left foot.

"*Ahh*, motherfucker!" That hurt like a bitch. I'm jumping around on the spot, cursing and rambling for a good three minutes, before I stop and shake my foot a little while inspecting the damage. Yep, that's going to bloody bruise all right.

"You might want to get on that little walkie thing and let Zac know that Reilly, get that name right, Reilly his new PR manager, is here." I can't help but give the brute attitude now. He slammed the goddamn door on my foot.

He steps aside, freeing the doorway. "Okay, sweetheart, settle down, come in and take a seat at the bar. I'll let him know you're here."

"Firstly, I'm Reilly, not your sweetheart or any other demeaning pet name you like to hand out, thinking it will make all of womankind swoon and forget you injured them. Secondly, I'll show myself to the bar, thank you."

I limp my way over to the bar. I'm almost there when the bartender from last night rounds the bar, stopping in front of me. James, I think his name was.

"What on earth happened to you?" he questions. Before I can answer, his hands are reaching out and grabbing me around my waist, effortlessly picking me up and placing me onto the bar. Great, Reilly, first day on the job and you're already sitting on top of the bar.

"The oaf at the door tried to slam said door in my face. I used my foot to stop it." I shrug my shoulders like it's no big deal.

James's eyes widen. "Kid has a bloody death wish," he mumbles, before telling me not to move.

39

I watch as James digs out a scoop of ice, wrapping it in a towel before making his way back to me. He's gentle as ever, picking up my injured foot and removing my shoe, then holds the ice onto my foot. I audibly moan at how good that ice feels right now.

"You're lucky I'm gay, sweets, or that moan right there would land you in a world of trouble, although…" Pausing, he looks me up and down. "Nope, still gay," he says, shaking his head.

"That's a damn shame to womankind, but if you ever want to really test that theory, hit me up, spunk," I say, waggling my eyebrows at him teasingly.

"I'm not stupid or crazy enough to test that out with you. I like breathing way too much," he responds.

I'm trying to process what he just said. I don't really get how I have anything to do with him breathing. Maybe he's been testing the product a bit under the bar.

"What the fuck is going on?" The deep, rough voice rumbles through me. Oh boy, I know that voice—my body was way too acquainted with that rumble last night. Just don't look up, Reilly. Don't make eye contact. Be strong. You do not need to get mixed up in his mess. Remember the cops rocking up on his doorstep this morning. And that right there does it; my resolve is set.

I look up to James, who looks like he's seen a ghost. He hands the ice over to Bray before saying, "I was just helping her, man. She injured her foot." Then he turns to me. "Sorry, sweets, you're on your own with this one. Like I said, I like breathing." James turns and practically runs out of the bar area.

I'm wiggling my ass closer to the edge, just about to jump down, when Bray puts a stop to my movements. Placing his hands on my knees, he says, "Don't even think about it, pumpkin." He then lifts my foot, inspecting the damage before gently placing the ice back on.

"How'd this happen?" he asks while his thumb rubs up and down the arch of my foot. Jesus, Holy Mother Mary. My body feels like a thousand bolts are currently running through it. Sparks. I can feel them everywhere. Is it hot in here? Oh man, I really need to get him to stop doing that. It's literally frying my brain.

Wait, he asked a question, right? I can do this—I can answer a question. I can jump down and release his hold on my foot. Deciding that's the best plan of action, I place my hands on his chest, on his well-defined muscle on top of muscle chest. Shoving him back slightly, I jump down.

"I tried to tell him that I was here to see Zac. He didn't believe me and went to shut the door in my face. My foot stopped the door. That's all, nothing too interesting. Now, is Zac in his office? Should I just head up there?" Lifting my head to meet his eyes, I can see he doesn't like what he heard. His face is stone and gives nothing away, but his eyes, they are brighter somehow, more intense than they were a minute ago.

"Wait, who the fuck slammed a fucking door on you?" he grunts out.

Okay, so maybe it's not just his eyes that are showing how mad he is. But what does he have to be mad about anyway? It was my bloody foot not his.

"You know, I didn't stop to get his name. Next time I see him around, I'll be sure to tell him Bray would like to know what your name is." Slipping my shoe back on, I walk around him and head to the lift that I remember leads to Zac's office. I can feel Bray's eyes on my back the whole damn way there. At least I'm not limping anymore, my foot feeling numb from the ice.

SITTING IN ZAC'S OFFICE, my mind is whirling with possibilities and ideas. I try to rein in my excitement and remain professional though. Zac is thorough, knows what he wants, and has high expectations for his club. I've been given the tour around the building, and shown where my office will be.

Notepad in hand, I'm currently sitting on the couch and taking copious notes of the many tasks he wants me to do. It's almost like he's challenging me, like he expects me to fail. Well, he's in for a rude awakening— Reilly Reynolds does not fail at anything. Well, maybe relationships, but that's mostly always intentional on my part.

"We host new and upcoming indie bands on Tuesdays and Thursdays. You'll notice in the calendar that we're currently booked for the month; you will have to start booking bands for the next month's spots." Zac is pacing his office as he rattles off task after task. Almost without taking a breath.

"We also host live bands on Fridays and Saturdays for limited time slots; the rest of the night is our featured DJs. I expect you to get to know them and work with them. Their contact details will be in your email contacts."

Finally, he takes a breather and pauses. Looking up at me, he squints his eyes, almost like there is something he's unsure of. Like he's trying to figure me out somehow. I sit and wait him out. I will not let his stare intimidate me. Straightening my spine, I arch an eyebrow at him, daring him to say something about me.

Zac just smirks at my silent challenge, asshole. "There are also *other* events we hold here. You won't need to do much for them. They promote themselves and are by invite only."

I didn't miss the way he said *other*. "What kind of other events, Zac?" I ask, my mind now whirling with worst-case scenarios. I can't stop my mouth before I start rambling on to him.

"Because if your *other* events are what I'm thinking, I'm walking out that door and keeping you far, far away from my best friend. Please, for the love of God tell me you are not auctioning off women. Prostitution? Oh boy, you're not selling drugs here, are you? No, you don't seem the type for that. Although, you think you know someone and then, *BOOM,* you really don't."

Zac is staring at me with scrunched up eyebrows. "What the fuck is wrong with you?" he asks before shaking his head. "Actually, don't answer that. No, I'm not running a goddamn woman auction or prostitution ring."

Just as he is about to say more, his phone starts blaring "My Girl" by The Temptations. When Zac answers the phone like his life depends on it, I can't help but laugh a little. Clearly that boy is lovesick.

I'm sitting here, trying not to be the nosy friend listening in on his conversation with Lyssa, but then he mentions roses and a card. He tells her that they are not from him. My blood goes cold and all that goes through my mind is that I need to get to her.

Alyssa is one of my best friends. I know her, and her past, and receiving flowers from an unknown sender is going to draw up unpleasant memories for her. Two years ago, one of Alyssa's old foster brothers started stalking her. She started receiving roses, odd gifts, and then the treats started. This went on for six months before he was finally caught when he attacked her in the hospital while she was doing her practical placement for college.

Reacting on autopilot, I jump out and grab the phone out of Zac's hand. I think he's so shocked by my sudden movements that he freezes for a moment. I have to push on his back to let him know to start moving as I talk to Alyssa. "Lyssa, it's Reilly. You are okay. You are safe. You're in

the hospital; nothing can happen to you in the hospital." I try to keep my voice as calm as I can manage in an attempt to reassure her.

"Lyssa, listen to me. Do not open that card. Don't touch it. We are on our way to you, okay? Zac and I, we're coming to get you, okay?"

Her voice is quiet as she agrees. Shit, this is not good. She's freaking out. I can tell by how quiet and shaky her voice is, her breathing quickening.

"I want you to stay on the phone with me until we get there. Go and tell whoever you need to tell that you're sick and you need to go home, okay?" I do everything I can to reassure her that it's not him. That she is not getting stalked again. I would know if he was released from jail.

Zac halts at the carpark and questions me. I can see he's stressed but I don't have time to deal with him right now. If Alyssa wants to share her past with him, that's up to her, not me.

"You need to drive. If you care about Alyssa at all, you need to get to the hospital now. Just know that she needs us. I can't tell you why, it's not my story to tell." It doesn't take him long to have the car screaming out of the carpark and towards the hospital.

I'm STANDING in Zac's apartment, correction Zac's penthouse, by myself wondering what the hell I do now. After collecting Alyssa up from the hospital bathroom floor, Zac threw his car keys at me and ordered me to drive. Let me repeat that, he ordered me to drive his Batmobile fancy-pants car because he wouldn't make Alyssa let go of him.

He carried her up to his apartment and then continued down a hallway, with me hot on his trail. He didn't even look behind him as he slammed what I'm assuming is his bedroom door. Deciding that Alyssa is actually in good hands with him, and that she seemed like she needed to be with him, I make my way back out to the living room, staring out of the floor-to-ceiling windows.

"What the hell do I do now?" I ask the city below.

Taking out my phone, I send a group message to Holly and Sarah, letting them know to get here as soon as they can. They both text back immediately that they are on their way. In my haste to get to Lyssa, I left my bag in Zac's office and my car at the club. Before thinking too much about it, I call Bray and he answers on the first ring.

"What's wrong?" he says in lieu of a greeting. "Nothing's wrong. Why does something have to be wrong for a girl to actually call you?"

"Babe, first, you're not a girl; you are all woman. Trust me, I've been up close and personal with your womanhood. I know. Second, women usually don't call me during the day; it's usually late at night. The only girl who ever calls me during the day is my little sister. So, I'll ask again, what's wrong?"

Damn it, why does the mention of other women calling him, clearly for booty calls, make my blood boil? I don't care who calls him for a damn booty call. If I say it enough, it's true, right? Choosing to be the bigger person and ignore his recall of last night's events, I tell him exactly why I'm calling, hoping to God that I can trust him enough to deliver my car to me in one piece.

"Okay, so the thing is, Zac and I had to go pick Lyssa up from work. Something happened and, in the rush out of Zac's office, I left—" I'm cut off by his booming voice on the other end of the phone.

"What the fuck happened to Lyssa? And why didn't you lead with that? Where is she now? I'm on my way!"

"Wait, Bray, Lyssa is fine. We are at Zac's apartment and she's holed up in the bedroom with him. I need you to get my bag from Zac's office—my car keys are in my bag. Can you please drive my car here?"

"No worries, babe, be there before you know it. Are you sure she's okay?" He sounds genuinely worried about her. I'm not entirely sure how to feel about that.

"Yes, she's fine. But you won't be if you even so much as put a scratch on my car. It's the black GT in the carpark."

"You drive a fucking Mustang? Be there soon. Oh, and don't make plans for tonight. You're busy." He hangs up before I can threaten him any further about damaging my car. Or tell him he's out of his mind if he thinks I'm busy with him tonight.

As I'm waiting for the girls, and now Bray, to show up, I come up with a genius plan to escape the building without Bray noticing it was me who was leaving. Well, not really genius since Holly and I have been trading places and fooling people all our lives. Nobody, other than our parents and closest friends, can ever tell when we've switched identities. I will be walking out of this building as Holly and not Reilly. By the time Bray notices, if he notices, I will be long gone.

# CHAPTER FOUR

*Bray*

*D*RIVING REILLY'S car to Zac's apartment is anything but a hardship. This car is a fucking dream. How the hell did Reilly end up with this? I know she's not long out of university, she's had one other job before Zac hired her, and that only just happened today.

The thought crosses my mind that a boyfriend or something bought it for her. That thought has me gripping the steering wheel tighter than necessary. I don't see Reilly as the type to take a gift like this from a bloke though. Maybe she's a trust fund baby—who the fuck knows? I'm damn sure going to find out everything there is to know about the fiery temptress.

Walking into Zac's apartment, it's more like walking into home. This is where we moved to after our parents died. Zac had already moved out of home and was living with Dean in the ultimate bachelor pad. When our parents died, his trust was opened, and he bought the penthouse, moving Ella and me in with him. He also bought the building of The Merge. At just 20 years old, he took on two teenagers and started up what is now the hottest nightclub in Sydney.

I couldn't be prouder that he's my brother; there isn't anything I wouldn't do for him. Knowing him, he would be silently losing his shit over something happening to Alyssa. I don't even know what the fuck happened yet and I'm stressed.

The living area is empty, so I make my way into the kitchen. Stopping at the doorway, I stay out of view, watching Reilly talking to Ella.

Taking Ella's hands in her own, she whispers, "Hunny, if you need help, I can help you. I promise. Who did this to you? Was it Zac? Bray?"

Her questions make me see red, as if Zac or I would ever lay a hand on a woman. Anyone that knows us knows there is nothing we wouldn't do for Ella. The guy who's currently worm food out in the Wollombi Forest would testify to that. If he was actually still breathing and could talk. It's that same guy who left those bruises on my sister's face. Just thinking about her being attacked like that makes me want to bring the asshole back to life just so I can watch the life drain from him again.

"I don't care how big or scary they are; I will hurt

whoever did this to you. This is not okay. You do not have to be treated like this! I'm taking you home with me; you don't have to worry about a thing."

Reilly continues to ramble. She's really getting herself worked up, which I find both amusing and something else I can't put my finger on. The fact that she's concerned over the welfare of my little sister and that she's willing to help her without a thought of herself is endearing, to say the least.

The look on Ella's face is fucking priceless. I can tell she doesn't know what to do. Scrunching her eyebrows up, she tries to convince Reilly that she's okay.

"Wait, you think that Zac or Bray would do this to me?

You know they're my brothers, don't you?"

"I don't care who they are; if they're responsible for this, I will have their balls in little glass jars sitting on my mantlepiece." Reilly says this so convincingly I actually believe she would attempt to cut my balls off.

Junior and I are both pretty well attached to said balls, and will not be parting with them anytime soon, ever if I can help it.

Ella looks mortified, so unsure how to handle the fiery siren standing before her. I know one way I'd like to handle her; unfortunately, it's not a viable option in front of my sister. I'm about to make myself known and put Ella out of her misery when she finally speaks up.

"Okay, you obviously don't know my brothers at all

if you think they are capable of doing this to me. I was attacked at The Merge. You can ask Lyssa. She's the one who bandaged me up afterwards." Ella's face is blank, like she's telling a story that she is totally detached from.

Not being able to handle seeing her this way, I walk into the kitchen. Not so quietly. Stomping my feet along the wooden floor, I make my way over to Ella and Reilly, stepping between the two so that my back is facing Reilly.

"There you are, sweetheart. I've been looking all over this damn castle for you," I say as I wrap Ella in my arms, placing a gentle kiss to her forehead. She immediately wraps her arms around my waist, settling her head on my chest.

I spin around with Ella still in my arms, my eyes landing on a shock-faced Reilly; although she's quick to recover and replace that shock with a scowl directed straight at me. Raising an eyebrow at her in question, she responds by stomping out of the kitchen. My eyes are immediately drawn to that perfect fucking heart-shaped ass of hers currently hugged by that tight skirt she's wearing.

I thought Reilly was fucking gorgeous in that skimpy club dress I tore off her last night. But that dress has nothing on work Reilly in her sexy librarian getup. *Mmm*, I wonder if I can get her to wear a pair of glasses with that outfit, while I bend her over a desk.

Stepping back from Ella, I clear my head of

thoughts of Reilly as I inspect the bruising on my little sister's face. I can't help the rage that comes over me when I see her like this.

Ella shakes out of my hold. "I'm fine, Bray. It doesn't even hurt that much anymore."

"You're my baby sister. You know I'm always going to worry about you."

Sighing as she begins to clean the already clean bench, Ella looks up at me. "I know and I appreciate that, but you really should worry about yourself. Now that Zac's practically married off to Alyssa, I think it's about time you look for someone stupid enough to put up with you, and lock that down. You don't want to be the eternal bachelor, do you?"

My eyes bug out of my head. Where the fuck is this coming from? Fucking Zac finding his one, that's where; and now it's given Ella ideas that I need the one too. Right on cue, an image of Reilly pops into my head.

"Don't worry your pretty little head about my love life, sis. Trust me, it's not lacking—that's for sure. But what about you? Any boys stupid enough to be hanging around?" I ask, knowing full well there is definitely something odd happening between her and Dean. I'm not sure what, and I trust Dean with her life, but there's an intensity I've seen from him towards Ella lately. I'm not sure if he wouldn't be stupid enough to try to go there with her.

"First, gross. I do not need to know who and how

many are warming your bed at night. Second, don't be stupid. You know I'd never tell you if there was a boy I fancied. It's way more fun sneaking around anyway." Ella smirks as she's about to walk out of the kitchen.

"Well, you might want to improve on your sneaking game, sis. It won't be long until Zac notices whatever the fuck is going on with you and Dean."

I watch as her back straightens and she misses a step. She's about to say something when Reilly walks back into the kitchen staring at her phone.

"Miss me already, babe?" I question her.

"Not in this lifetime," she replies as she turns to Ella, who is currently bobbing her head between the two of us.

I see the moment the lightbulb goes off in her head, and a huge-ass grin spreads across her face. "This is gonna be soooooo good," Ella says excitedly.

"No idea what's going to be good, but Zac asked me to get Lyssa some food. Correction, Zac ordered me to get Lyssa some food," Reilly tells Ella.

Just then the phone she is still clutching starts beeping in her hand. "Shit, the girls are here. I need to run down and let them in."

"Don't worry. I'll get Lyssa a plate of food; you go let them in. You'll have to take a lift card with you to get back up."

I'm watching the dynamic between Ella and Reilly and am in awe how quickly Ella is taking to her. Not that there's much to not like. I mean, damn, just looking at her and I have to adjust junior to give him more room for the growing he's doing right now.

"Wait, you said girls? I'll go let them up for you," I offer, giving her my best smirk.

Reilly looks me up and down, and I can see the fury in those green eyes of hers that she's trying so damn hard to hide. "Not a damn chance, pretty boy," she exclaims as she storms out.

Ella laughs. "Way to get shut down, bro. I think I like her."

"What's not to like?" I ask. Not waiting for a response, I make my way into Zac's office; that's where he hides the good liquor.

AFTER I'VE SLAMMED BACK two shots of whisky, I start making my way back out to the living room in search of Dean, only to stop in my tracks at the sound of voices—Reilly's not so quiet whisper to her friends to *shut it*.

I know I probably shouldn't, but I can't help but stop and eavesdrop on the conversation between Reilly and her friends. That is until I hear one of her friends announce, "If you don't want to ride that pierced cucumber again, I'll take it for a spin."

Reilly responds with, "Go for it, see if I care."

That's when I decide to make myself known. "See if you care about what, pumpkin?" I ask, wrapping an arm around her shoulder.

An arm which she's very quick to shrug off. Ignoring her shrug, I turn my full-watt smile onto her sister and her friend.

"Ladies, it's good to see you again."

"Oh no, the pleasure is all mine. I'm Sarah, in case you forgot," Sarah says as she takes a step closer to me.

I look across to Reilly, raising my eyebrows in question. Is her friend seriously trying to hit on me right now? Reilly's oblivious to my question though, currently staring daggers at Sarah. Well, that's an interesting turn of events.

Thinking I could play on her sudden green-eyed monster, I turn and give Sarah the full look over, up and down, then back up and down again. You would have to be blind to say she's not hot as fuck. My mind is telling me she's a ten; however, junior is not budging, not even slightly.

*Huh*, well, there goes that idea. Either Reilly broke junior last night or he just really knows what he wants right now. And I have a feeling what he wants is the fiery redhead standing next to me.

Leaning down into her ear and ensuring her friends can hear, I say, "You can put the claws away, pumpkin. It seems junior has his sights set exclusively on you."

Reilly's mouth gapes open and closed for a few seconds before she straightens her shoulders and replies, "Junior is going to be feeling very lonely if he doesn't find a friend to play with, because I most certainly will not be reacquainting myself with him."

"Sure, we'll have to agree to disagree with that, babe," I say as I walk away, continuing my search to find where the fuck Dean's hiding out.

# CHAPTER FIVE

*Reilly*

"*I* CAN'T BELIEVE Zac called us out like that. How on earth could he tell, Rye? No one has ever been able to tell us apart without knowing us before," Holly says as she's stares at her reflection in the lift mirror.

She's in a tizzy because I talked her into changing clothes and pretending to be me so I could walk out of the apartment as Holly, escaping the likes of Bray and his pierced cucumber. It turns out I didn't have to worry about it, because when we walked out of Zac's bedroom, Bray was nowhere to be seen.

"Well, it doesn't matter now anyway. Bray left before us, which means crisis averted."

"Tell me again, if that pierced cucumber of his was so magical, then why are you avoiding it?"

She knows damn well why I need to stay away from that one. She just wants me to admit it, which is never going to happen, ever. Trying to play down the effect that he has over me, I shrug my shoulders at her as we exit the lift. "It wasn't that good."

I'm lying and I know she knows it. It wasn't just good… it was the best damn cucumber I've ever bloody had. And that right there, that is why I can't let myself get attached, that is why I need to stay far, far away from…

My thoughts are interrupted by Holly's gasp. Noticing she's not right next to me anymore, I turn around only to come face to face with a shocked and frozen Holly, currently wrapped in a pair of very muscular tattooed arms. Damn it, Reilly, get your head in the game. You are not Reilly right now you are Holly.

And if Holly can just pull it together long enough for us to get out of here, that'd be great. I'm not liking my chances—by the way she looks like a mouse caught by the bloody cat.

"Trying to run out on me, babe?" Bray says into Holly's neck.

Shit, shit, shit, Holly looks like she's about to pee herself. As I'm racking my brain for a way to get us out of this, Bray curses and spins Holly around to face him.

He looks between the two of us, back and forward a couple of times, before he smirks at me—a smirk that makes my ovaries shiver. Before I know what's happening, Bray storms up to me, grabs my face between both of his hands and lands his lips on mine.

I'm doing my best to resist, to not open my mouth for him. He's damn well persistent though. And those lips, those full soft lips of his just feel so bloody good. I can't help the moan that escapes as he brushes his tongue along the seam of my lips.

For a moment, I give in, returning the kiss just as eagerly as he is giving it. Everything around me fades, and all of my senses are zoned into all that is Bray. His exotic, masculine, earthy scent surrounding me, making me feel like I've been whisked away to the forest. What I wouldn't do to have this man throw me up against a tree trunk right now, the bark scratching at my back as he thrusts into me.

"*Umm*, Rye, I guess I'll just meet you at home."

Holly's voice snaps me out of my Bray-induced insanity. That's what he does to me, makes me insanely freaking horny and forget everything else. Pushing back, I step away from Bray, who is just staring at me with the biggest smirk on his face. Which just adds fuel to my growing fire now.

"What the hell, Bray?" I ask, crossing my arms over my chest. It then occurs to me that I'm Holly right now. Did he think he was kissing Holly?

"Why the fuck are you trying to kiss my sister?" I question.

His eyebrows draw in like he doesn't understand the question. I can tell the minute the lightbulb goes off in his mind, because outcomes that full-watt smile again. Look away from the smile, Reilly. Do not let that delectable mouth draw you in again.

"Babe, I was not trying to kiss your sister." Looking over at Holly, he says, "Not that you're not smoking hot, Holl, because obviously you are."

"*Umm*, thanks?" Holly questions, going beet red. She does not take compliments from men as easily as I do.

"Why'd you switch clothes anyway?" Bray asks me. "That's on a need-to-know basis, and you do not need

to know. Now, if you'll excuse us, we need to get going." I try to step around him, only to have him wrap his arm around my waist, stopping me.

"Not so fast, buttercup. I need a ride home," he says as his thumb trails circles on my waist. Why does his simple touch affect me like this? Just his hand on my waist is creating a storm of tingly sensations that run through me. I'm not even going to mention the effect it's having on my panties. I really need to get away from him.

"Not my problem, call an Uber. You have heard of them, right?" Internally, I am telling myself to stay strong. *Do not let him affect you, Reilly. This will not end well for you.*

"It became your problem when you asked me to drive your car here, babe. So, stop arguing and let's go."

Bray takes hold of my hand, like he has every right

to, like it belongs to him somehow. It feels good to have my hand in his, warm, safe even. But no, I am not falling for that. Pulling my hand away, and shaking out the tingles, I find I'm still walking next to him. I think I may have lost my mind.

Bray stops suddenly, spinning around. "Holly, how are you getting home? Do you need a ride?"

One could be fooled that he is actually concerned about how my sister is getting home. I am not *one*.

"No, I'm fine, thanks. I have my car here," Holly says as she points to her yellow VW out on the street. I watch as Bray looks at the car then back to Holly.

"Wait here a minute, babe," he says as he takes Holly's bag from her and proceeds to walk her out to her car, waiting for her to get in before he turns to make his way back inside.

Okay, well, that was... I don't know what the hell that was. I do know we need to clear up this whole *babe* thing though. I swear my bloody ovaries do a little flip every time they hear him say the word.

"You ready, sweet cheeks?" Bray asks as he takes my hand again, only for me to pull it out of his hold, again.

"Sweet cheeks? No, just no. And while we're on the subject of pet names, I am not now—and I am not ever going to be—your babe, your buttercup or your damn pumpkin. My name's Reilly. Start using it!" I am almost yelling by the end of my rant.

The asshole laughs; that's right, he laughs at me. "Just another thing for us to agree to disagree on. You know you're cute as fuck when you get all worked up?"

"*Argh*, just show me where my car is. And there better not be a scratch on her."

"Sure, *Reilly*, this way. It's in the basement." He puts extra emphasis on my name. I thought him not using pet names would be easier on the ovaries, but I was wrong, very, very wrong.

BRAY GIVES me directions to his house and I stop at the gate, waiting for him to get out. He just sits there staring at me. It's making me self-conscious. Do I have something on my face? I'm pretty sure I don't.

"You know, this is usually the part where you say thanks for the ride, Reilly. Catch you around," I tell him, hoping to get him out of my car.

"*Huh*. You know, I'd be happy to give you a ride you'd be thanking me for," he says as he waggles his eyebrows up and down at me. Before I can respond—

because yes, it takes a bit for my mind to stop playing images of just what kind of ride he is offering—he snaps me out of my thoughts. "Wind your window down and enter the code, babe. It's 2501."

Like the idiot I am, I do just that: wind my window down, enter the code and drive through the gates as they open. At this point I think it's my ovaries leading me to my doom. Stopping the car at the end of his driveway, I tell him, "Okay, you're home. You can get out now."

Laughing, he shakes his head at me. "I have your purse thingy you left here last night. You wanna come in and grab it?"

I do want to get that clutch; it has my cards in it. But is it worth the risk of entering his house again? I'm not sure. "Can't you just run in and get it and bring it back out to me?" I plead with him.

"Are you afraid that friendly vagina of yours ain't gonna be able to stop wanting to play with junior if you step inside?"

What the... wait, did he really just say that? "My friendly vagina? Really, Bray? Trust me, it's not as friendly as you think. Right now, the right name would be bitchy vagina and the last thing my vagina wants to do is play with junior now or ever!" If I keep saying it, we both might actually start believing it.

"Well, babe, your vagina was plenty friendly to junior last night. I can't help it if he thinks he's found his new playmate. Also, you can't really say he doesn't have good taste, because I can still taste that friendly vagina of yours and I'm starving for another feed."

Holy shit, well, how the hell do I respond to that? God damn it, now my vagina really does want to play, or be played.

"It's not happening, Bray. Please, I really need to go home. I can just get my clutch another time, or you can bring it to the club or something." I can't even make eye contact with him as I practically beg him not to make me go inside.

Bray's silent for a moment as he looks at me, then he shocks me by holding my face, bringing my eyes to meet his. "Reilly, you know I'd never make you do something you don't want to do, right?"

I nod my head because, somehow, I do feel safe with him. I do feel like he would never hurt me. But it's the unpredictable nature of life that will end up hurting me. It's the cops banging on the door at all hours of the morning and taking him off in handcuffs—that's what will hurt me.

"Okay, wait here. I'm going to run in and grab your things." Before getting out of the car, he leans in and kisses my forehead.

Kisses on the forehead are kryptonite. Jesus, why does he have to be so damn perfect? It takes less than two minutes for him to come running back out of the house holding my clutch and some garment bags.

He opens the passenger side door, places the clutch

on the seat and then lays the garment bags across the back seat.

"What's with those?" I ask, pointing to the bags.

"I told you I'd replace the dress I ripped, so I did." He shrugs.

"*Uhh,* thanks?" I don't mean it to come out as a question but it does. "You do realise there are two bags there, don't you? You only ripped one dress."

"I know, and I fully intend on ripping this particular dress again, next time I see you wearing it. That's why there's two. Now when I rip the new dress, you already have another one." He ends with a wink.

I actually think he's serious right now. "You're not going to be ripping any dresses off me again, Bray. Sorry, but you wasted your money."

"Agree to disagree, babe, that seems to be becoming a thing for us. Drive safe, and text me or call me when you get home." He doesn't let me respond before shutting the door and walking into his house.

Well, I hope for his sake he is a patient man. Because he's going to be waiting a long time for that text to come.

ONE WEEK. I have managed to work at The Merge for a whole week without having to run into Bray once. I've dodged corners, and hidden out in bathrooms to achieve this, but achieve it I have.

I've gotten to know a lot of the staff here. The bar staff is great, especially James. He and I are going to be great friends. The security staff on the other hand is hard to read. Other than Dean, they all seem to avoid me like the plague. Whenever I go to talk to any of them or try to ask them something, they mumble under their breaths and make an excuse that they have to go. Dean is always quick to come and find me to see what it is I need. I mean, it's not that I don't like Dean. I do. It's just hella weird. I've never had men avoid me like this; usually it's the other way around, like me avoiding Bray for instance.

"Reilly, are you listening?" Zac asks.

*Oh shit.* Yep, totally zoned out while I was in a meeting with Zac. I should be jotting down all the notes and the endless list he wants me to do.

"Sorry, I must have missed that. What'd you say?" I try for my sweet, butter wouldn't melt voice. It gets me absolutely nowhere with Zac though. He is a man on a mission. He knows what he wants and goes for it. I actually respect the hell out of him, but I will go to my grave before I ever admit that.

I admire the business side of him. The way he has built this business up from the ground and at such a young age is admirable. Again, I'm never admitting that to anyone.

"Well, if you're done daydreaming, and please do refrain from sharing whatever thoughts had you pre-occupied, I need you to go to the store and get a dress," he says.

This has my attention. I don't know whether I should be pissed off, or excited at this point. Pissed off, because I am not his bloody personal shopper, and excited because shopping and Zac's credit card seem like one hell of a good time.

"First, I am not your personal shopper. Second, prepare to lose your balls if that dress you want me to buy is not for Alyssa." I glare at him for extra measure.

He scrunches his eyebrows up. "First, you're my employee, under my employ. If I ask you to run an errand, that's what you'll do. Second, who the hell else do you think I'd be buying a fucking dress for?"

"Good answer, but why do you need to buy Lyssa a dress?" It seems like an odd request, even from him. Trust me, I've had some odd requests over the week.

"There's a fight tonight after her shift. She's coming, and I'm guessing that she's not going to want to go out into the club or down to the basement in her scrubs."

"You're actually going to take her down to the basement? I haven't even seen this exclusive basement yet. If I buy the dress, I'm coming to the fight."

"I don't have a choice. I have to be there—it's the last fight of the year. And I'm sure as fuck not going to leave Alyssa up here by herself." Standing, he takes a black card from his wallet and hands it over.

"Here, buy something suitable, but make sure it actually covers her. I don't need all the fuckers down there to be staring at what's mine," he says, like I'm going to listen to a word of that.

Inspecting the fancy black card, I ask, "Is there a limit on this bad boy?"

"No, make sure you get her shoes as well, and be back by nine. The fight starts at nine thirty tonight, and I have a feeling that you're not going to want to miss it."

"Are you serious? I've been waiting all week to see what happens down there. I'll be back." As I'm walking out of his office, the pierced cucumber walks in. I mean Bray, Bray walks in. Wearing a pair of sweats, nothing else. And there go the ovaries again. Doing my best not to be obviously checking him out, I hurry out of the office and get the hell out of the building. I think I'll enjoy this little shopping trip.

Just one glance at Bray, and I need to recalibrate my

system into the *I don't want Bray Williamson or junior, his pierced cucumber,* mentality. I'm probably the only woman on earth to ever mutter that sentence.

ONE HELL of a shopping trip later, I'm standing next to one very excited Alyssa and one very pissed at me Zac. Let's just say he was not impressed with the dress I picked out for her; but damn, she is owning that dress. Her body is killer and she has curves in all the right places. It's a crime not to show it off.

The crowd down here is pumped. We've watched a few fights already and are apparently waiting for the main event. Although no one will comment on who the fighters are in the main event. The cage has just been cleaned out after the last fighters.

I'm not surprised that even down here, in this underground fight club, Zac has everything running like a fine-tuned machine. All of a sudden, the lights go dark, then a spotlight shines at the fighter's entrance and "T.N.T." by ACDC blasts from the speakers.

I strain my neck to see who this fighter is that's coming out. I really, really shouldn't have looked. Of course, he has to be a fucking cage fighter. Walking out with two women wearing just bikinis, one hanging off each side of him, is no other than Bray fucking Williamson.

He comes out wearing I guess what he is passing off as a pair of black shorts, though they look more like painted on boxer briefs. His whole body is on display for all to see; those two skanky card girls in bikinis sure are getting their fill.

Bray is dancing and playing it up to the crowd. And although those girls try to get up and rub all over him, I do smile a little when I see him shake his head no at them and move them back an inch. *Huh, that's interesting.* The bikini girls look just as shocked as I am at the turn of events. Bray steps into the cage, and I'm ashamed to say that my eyes haven't strayed too far from him the whole time he's been dancing his way out here.

Looking to Lyssa standing next to me, I can tell straight away something is wrong. She's panicked, looking all around the room. Zac is holding her like his life depends on it; his face is as stern and furious as I've ever seen it.

"What's wrong?" I yell over the noise of the crowd.

He doesn't say anything, just hands me Lyssa's

phone with a message open on it. My blood goes cold when I see the message. This cannot be happening to her again. I don't know how she can survive living through another stalker coming at her like this.

YOU SHOULDN'T TOUCH *things that don't belong to you! He was mine first. I saw him first! I won't warn you again, bitch. He is MINE. He will be with me again, even if I have to take you out myself. xxx*

I FEEL HELPLESS. I don't know what to do right now. I look back to the cage and my eyes land on Bray. He's staring at me, eyes squinted. He looks like he's ready to jump back out of the cage. Then he looks at Zac and nods before indicating to the ref that he's ready.

I watch Bray's movements, unable to take my eyes off him. My heart feels like it stops as the bell rings to begin the fight. It seems like only seconds later Bray's opponent is on the ground, knocked out cold from one hit. Bray leaps out of the cage, ignoring the calls from the crowd and heads straight for us. Straight for me.

He wraps his arm around me, and I let him. I soak up the comfort that he's offering and take everything I can. He says something to Zac and Dean before guiding me along with the rest of our group out of the basement. He doesn't let go and I honestly don't think I want him to right now. That text message even freaked me out, and I don't scare easily.

I'm not scared for myself. I'm scared for my best friend. I'm scared for how this is going to affect her. I know what she needs. What she needs right now is her girls—this calls for a slumber party of the most epic proportions. Lots of alcohol, snacks and more alcohol will be consumed tonight.

# CHAPTER SIX

*Bray*

I'VE JUST CLIMBED into bed, in my old bedroom in Zac's penthouse. I don't really stay here often but he has never changed my room from when I moved out a few years back.

I sat out in the living room for hours listening to the girls laugh and squeal. I'm glad they could help Alyssa relax and try to forget about that fucking psycho Caitlyn sending her those damn messages. I want to fucking strangle that bitch. If she thinks she can hurt my family, she can think again. I will stop at nothing to protect them, and Alyssa is now a part of that.

I know Reilly likes to put on a tough persona, but I've been watching her this past week. I've purposely stayed out of her way, much to the disappointment of junior. The way she looked so broken and stressed in the car when she dropped me off, I know she's struggling with something. As much as I'd like to help her, I also don't want to make things harder for her.

I hear the rattle of my doorknob turning or attempting to turn. I'm about to jump out of bed, ready and alert, when I see those long legs paired with a mop of red hair tumbling into the room. At this moment, I'm really fucking hoping that it's Reilly and not Holly stumbling in here.

It's too hard to tell in the dark. I'd have to touch whoever it is to find out. When I wrapped my arms around Holly a week ago, I knew straight away that something was off. I didn't get that electric sense running through me. My body didn't feel as alive as it does whenever I touch Reilly. That was the first sign that they had switched clothes. The second was the green-eyed monster Reilly, who was dressed as and portraying Holly, was throwing my way.

I watch as this gorgeous redhead stumbles and curses. "Fuck, shit, fuck."

Thank Christ, that is definitely Reilly. I watch as she stumbles her way through the room. There is just enough light coming from the en-suite that I can make out her features. It is also very clear that she's shit-faced right now. A fact that junior is not happy about. I may be a bastard, but I have never and will never take advantage of an intoxicated woman.

I'm silent as I watch her fumble with the zip of her dress. When she finally manages to get the zip down all the way, she just lets the thing fall to the floor. Holy Mother of God, she is standing—okay, she's more swaying—but she is swaying in only a pair of panties. She's been braless all fucking night. Damn it, I need to get junior under control. He's not understanding that it's not time for him to come out and play.

Reilly pulls the sheet back and climbs into the bed, falling half on top of me. It's at this moment she notices she's not alone in the room.

"*Ahh*, what the hell?" She attempts to jump back out of bed, but I don't let her get far. Wrapping an arm around her, I hold her close to me. Reilly does not like this one bit; she tries landing punches on my chest. I really need to get her in a gym and teach her how to actually hit more effectively. I can't help but chuckle at her attempts.

Stopping her fight, she questions, "Bray?"

"Yeah, babe, it's me. Who the fuck else did you think you were getting into bed with naked?" The thought of her getting into bed naked with any other mother-fucker pisses me right the fuck off.

"*Umm*, no one, I thought... Ella told me this room would be empty." She sighs, as she snuggles in closer to me. I know, if it wasn't for the alcohol, there is no way she would be snuggling up to me. But am I going to turn away her snuggles? Fuck no, I've never claimed to be a saint and she is a sin I am more than prepared to indulge in.

"Ella sent you in here?" I ask, wondering what my

sister is up to, since she knew I was staying the night. Looks like Ella is playing little miss matchmaker. I'll have to send her a huge bloody thank you card for this match.

"*Uh-huh*, I can go. I'm sure there are plenty of surfaces in this castle I can sleep on," she says, making no move to actually move.

"You're not sleeping anywhere else, sweetheart. You're right where you're meant to be."

She looks up at me and fans her fingers down my face, that electric zap very much alive and coursing through my body.

"I really wish I could let myself have you, Bray." I guess a drunk Reilly is an honest Reilly, good to know.

"You already have me, whether you want me or not, babe." I doubt she will remember any of this conversation in the morning, so I may as well lay all my cards out on the table, my balls along with them.

Reilly shakes her head. "No, I can't have you. You see, I made a promise a long, long, longggg time ago," she slurs.

"What promise?"

"That I wouldn't end up like her."

"Like who?" What the fuck happened to her that she can't let herself be happy?

"I can't tell you. But I'm not strong like her. I can't do it. I'm sorry. I really would have liked for you to be mine." She leans up inches from my mouth, about to kiss me. I stop her. It pains me to do so, but I know how wasted she is, and I can't let her do something she will likely regret, well, any more than she already has.

"Go to sleep, babe. I'm not doing anything with you while you're intoxicated. The next time your friendly vagina and junior have a playdate, you're going to be sober and clear-headed."

Reilly scrunches her face up at me. "What? Why? I am clear-headed; I know what you can do with that pierced cucumber of yours and I want you to do it to me. Now, Bray!"

I can't hold the laughter, and when I finally calm myself down, it's evident that she is not impressed by my outburst.

"Pumpkin, you can have this pierced cucumber, anytime, anywhere…" I get down real close to her face, our lips barely millimetres away. "When. You're. Sober."

"*Argh*, you and I both know I'm not going to want your pierced cucumber anywhere near me when I'm sober." Reilly pouts, full on lips sticking out pout. It's fucking adorable. It's taking everything I've got not to lean in and kiss her.

"Agree to disagree, babe. You're going to want to play with junior. You just won't admit it, to me or yourself. There is a difference," I tell her as I position her body so she's snuggled up to my side. My arm is underneath her head, allowing it to rest on my shoulder, her long, red tresses sprawled out behind her. She's so fucking perfect.

I kiss her forehead. "Go to sleep, Reilly. You're likely to feel like shit when you wake up as it is; you don't want to be sleep-deprived as well."

"Thank you, Bray. I know I'll probably regret saying this tomorrow, but you are one of the good ones," she says as she snuggles in.

I doubt I'm going to get a wink of sleep tonight; junior is fucking raging hard, not that I can blame him. I have a practically naked Reilly in my arms. What I need to do is come up with a plan to figure out exactly what Reilly is afraid of. What the fuck happened to make her so jaded? If I can figure that out and know what I'm fighting against, the odds will be in my favour —because one thing I don't do is lose a fucking fight. I have a feeling that the fight for Reilly will be the hardest, but most rewarding one yet.

I'M in the kitchen making coffee, while trying to decide how to make Reilly's coffee. How do I not already know how she takes her coffee? I've been watching her all week. I've seen her drinking it every day as she enters the club.

I'm debating between a cappuccino and that sweet latte shit that Alyssa drinks. Why the fuck am I so stressed about coffee anyway? She either likes it or doesn't like it. I'm just about to make a decision when Holly appears in the kitchen.

"Thank fuck you're up. How the hell does your sister take her coffee?" I ask her.

She seems a little thrown off kilter, as she stares at me with wide eyes. *"Umm, uhh,"* she mumbles before finally telling me, "she just has straight black, nothing fancy."

Straight black, I can do. Turning, I hit the button telling the machine to pour a long black.

*"Umm,* Bray…" Holly's timid voice grabs my attention. It's hard to believe she and Reilly are twins; besides looks, the two couldn't be more different.

"Yeah?" I question with a raised eyebrow.

"How do you always manage to tell Reilly and me apart so easily? I mean, I didn't even say anything when I walked in, and you knew it was me and not Reilly."

"Well, you guys might look the same, but your mannerisms are complete opposites. You also have that little freckle under your left eye where Reilly doesn't." I shrug like it's not a big deal. Then I remember the main thing that helps me know them.

"Oh, also, I don't get the same electric feel from you

that I do from Reilly. When I look at you, junior is not aching to come out to play. But when I look at Reilly, he is bursting at the seams to play with her, literally." I wink.

I watch as Holly processes what I just said; it clicks in and her face screws up. "*Eww*, wait, you really call your *you know what* junior? Also, Reilly and I look just the same, so why does junior like Reilly and not me?" she says as she points to my dick, while also silencing the insistent beeping coming from her phone.

I laugh at her unease. I know I shouldn't but she's fucking cute. "Holl, surely you've had boyfriends. All guys have a name for their dicks. And I can't explain why junior jumps for Reilly but not you. I'm not saying you're not hot as fuck, Holly. Obviously you are. I just look at you and see a sister. I look at Reilly and see, well, you get the picture."

She shrugs her shoulders up and down. "I have had a couple of boyfriends, but none of them have had names for their, you know." She gestures to my crotch area.

"Trust me, Holl, they had names. They just didn't tell you."

Holly's phone continues to beep and she continues to silence it.

"You know a good way to get people to stop messaging is to answer them. You and your sister both need to learn how to answer messages." I lean against the bench and wait for her response as she looks down at her phone again, only to silence it once more. Her face screws up a little. I've noticed both twins make this exact same face while thinking.

"I can't answer it until I talk to Reilly. I need her help with something. Speaking of, where is my sister?"

"She's asleep still. What do you need help with? Maybe I can help you?" I offer, because there is no way in hell I'm letting anyone drag Reilly out of my bed this morning.

"Unless you're prepared to find yourself tagging along on a double date with me and this guy, you can't help," she says as she waves her phone in front of her.

"Babe, I don't usually have any issue finding a date. When is this double date?" I ask. It then dawns on me that she was planning on asking Reilly to go on this date, which means Reilly would have taken someone, that same someone not being me.

Before she can answer, I'm jumping on her. "Wait a fucking second, you were going to get Reilly to go on this double date thing with you?"

"Well, yeah, she always comes with me on dates. Not that I date much, but if I do, she tags along. Why?" She smirks at me knowingly.

*Huh*, guess I walked into that one. But I don't fucking care. I smirk back.

"Sign us both up to tag along. Reilly and I are going to be your date buddies. Who's the guy anyway?"

"Oh, he's the physical education teacher from school. He's been asking me out for a while now and I keep saying no. I figured I'd say yes one time and see what happens." She shrugs, then adds, "Good luck telling Reilly she's going to be your date," as she exits the room laughing.

REILLY IS STILL out of it on my bed when I make my way back into the room. Placing the coffees on the dresser, I stand against the wall, debating whether I should wake her or not. I decide on the not; this may be the only chance I get to peacefully look my fill without her giving me a death glare in return. The fact that the sheets have dropped to her waist, displaying all of her glorious breasts, helps this decision.

What I wouldn't do to get my mouth, hands, anything on those breasts. Damn, my junior is roaring to go at them too. Something tells me she would not welcome the ideas I have of just how I could wake her, how I want to wake her every fucking morning.

Shit, where the hell are these thoughts coming

from? I really do need to get laid. The only issue is junior; he has not even budged at another woman since meeting Reilly. The bastard is fucking hooked on her, loyal to her.

"Are you going to stand there all day staring like a creeper, Bray? Or are you actually going to hand me that coffee I can smell."

Reilly's sleepy voice draws me out of my own head. "I'll take option one, babe; I could stare at you all day and not tire of the view. I'll let you creep on me as much as you want to because as you know, I'm a giver like that." I raise my eyebrows suggestively at her.

Reilly slowly sits up, pulling the sheet up and covering those breasts I haven't been able to stop staring at. "*Argh*, God, make yourself useful and pass me that coffee, Bray," she says as she rubs her temples.

Like a fucking lost little puppy, I do exactly that. I pick up her coffee and walk it over, holding it out to her. She snaps it up and within seconds is moaning as she sips on the hot brew. Even doing a simple thing like drinking coffee, she takes my breath away; she is fucking gorgeous.

"Okay, your staring is actually starting to creep me out a little here. You might want to tone it down a bit," she says while staring at my crotch. My ever-growing fucking crotch that is on full display in these loose-fitting shorts.

"It's not my fault you're so damn beautiful to look at. You know junior is your number one fan, babe. I can't control what he likes." I make a point of looking down and waving at junior. "You know, if you were a real friend, you'd help a mate out here," I suggest.

Reilly laughs, "We are not friends, Bray, not even close.

Now, turn around so I can get dressed."

"Ouch, that hurts, sweets," I lament, holding my hand over my heart. I walk into the closet and pick up a shirt for her. "Put this on. What are your plans for today?" I ask, making a point of not turning around while she slips the shirt over her head.

"I'm going shopping with Alyssa. Why?" "What about tonight?" I ask.

"Washing my hair." She shrugs.

"How about you come to my place and I'll help you wash your hair," I suggest.

"Not going to happen. Sorry." She stands up and starts looking around the room. "Have you seen my phone?"

I walk over to the dresser and pick up her now fully- charged phone, handing it to her. "I charged it for you."

Reilly tilts her head, mouth open, and seems stunned. She's quick to recover herself as she takes the phone, mumbling out a thanks.

She's staring down at her phone and is just about to the door when she suddenly stops, spinning around and looking straight up at me.

"Why the hell is Holly saying we are double dating

tomorrow night? And by we, I mean you and me?" she says, pointing between me and her.

I smile. I'm finally going to get her out on a date. "Your sister asked me to help her out. She has this date with some PE teacher from her school. She seemed sceptical, almost like she didn't even want to go out with the guy. I didn't like it and I'm not about to let her go alone. I'm a good friend like that. I help my mates out."

Reilly rolls her eyes. "Whatever, I wouldn't have let her go alone anyway." She then walks out the door, slamming it behind her.

# CHAPTER SEVEN

*Reilly*

HY DO I continue to get myself into these situations? I have barely slept all night, trying to wrap my head around just how I'm going to get through a whole date with Bray tonight. Luckily, it's a double date with Holly and that creepy-ass Simon, the PE teacher from her school.

I've met Simon before, a couple of times when I've been out with Holly and she's ran into him. The guy gives me the creeps. I can't point my finger on what it is, but I just get those vibes from him. If Holly's date was with anyone else, I probably would have fought the whole Bray tagging along thing and found myself someone else to go with.

I'll never admit this to anyone, but I do feel a weird sense of peace knowing that Bray will be there. I have no doubt that he would come across as intimidating and protective of Holly while in the company of her creepy date. Why the hell she's even agreed to go out with him, I will never know. But because she's my sister and I love her, and the fact that she dates only once in a blue moon, I will go along with this shamble of a date tonight.

First, I need to find some inner grounding. I need to rebuild the walls back up around my damn heart. Every time I get a glimpse of Bray, another brick comes tumbling down, letting him seep into places he has no business being. I've spent the last five years mortaring and rendering those bricks to ensure they are firmly in place. I'm not about to let Bray bulldoze them down.

I need a plan, a bloody good one to survive a whole night with his torture. Yesterday was bad enough. I spent the day shopping with Alyssa, Sarah, Holly and Ella, and guess who Zac made tag along with us? Yep, you guessed it, Bray fucking Williamson. I had to endure a whole day of his constant charm and good fucking looks.

I don't understand how one person can be as blessed in the looks department as that asshole is. The whole day he was constantly next to me, or close enough that I could smell him. I thought I was going crazy; I was turned on the whole damn day and by the looks he kept giving me, he knew what his close proximity was doing to me.

Then there was the whole dressing room scene.

Some bastard slipped through all of us unnoticed, managing to slip a picture under the door of the dressing room Alyssa was in. The soul-piercing scream that came from behind her door is still ringing in my head. I cannot get that sound out of my thoughts. I've never been so scared for one of my friends in all my life.

Sarah and I both tried to get her to open the door for us. Bray came running in from the front of the store and straight away got her to open the door, only to then push himself into the room with Alyssa and shut the door behind them. I felt a strange mixture of jealousy and a calmness at that.

I was jealous that he was in a dressing room with my friend while she was in her underwear, my bloody hot as sin friend. At the same time, as I listened to him talk to her, I heard him coaxing her into her clothes on the other side of the door and talking her out of her panic. I felt a sense of calmness and relief that my friend had some great people in her corner. She needs this; she needs people like the Williamsons in her life.

We spent the rest of the afternoon in a wine bar. I may have had a little too much to drink, again. I had Holly take me home earlier than everyone else with the excuse that we had a family thing to do. Sarah and Alyssa both knew that we were bullshitting. They know of our shitty family circumstances. They know the only family we have now is our mum. We both still live at home with her, neither of us wanting to leave her alone.

She's strong, probably one of the strongest women I know, to survive the last five years how well she has. She picked herself up off of that courtroom floor five years ago and dusted off her dress, straightened her shoulders and told both Holly and me that we would be fine. That we would get through this together.

And survive we did. We have a great relationship and usually I talk to her about everything. But I've been holding back talking to her about Bray, partly because I know what she's going to say. She'll tell me to open my heart to the possibility. That the best thing that ever happened to her was meeting my dad. Even today, she has stayed loyal to him. He's facing at least another ten years in jail, but my mum is waiting. She won't even contemplate moving on.

She won't visit him in jail. She says that her heart hurts too much to see him locked up like an animal. They write to each other every day and that's how they have managed to stay connected all these years.

I'LL BE SEEING my dad today. Maybe he can help talk me out of these stupid feelings I'm catching. I'm the only one who visits my dad. On the first Sunday of each month, I make my trek down to the Silverwater Correctional Facility. I make a day of it, first visiting my dad and then my brother to tell him all about what's been happening.

Deciding this is exactly the day I need in order to re- ground my inner self, I throw the blankets off and get moving. First coffee, then shower, then car. I mentally give myself a list to get on with. I will not think of the pierced cucumber or the body and mind that come with that pierced cucumber today.

Which is a shame. I really would like to be better friends with junior—we could be best friends. Maybe Bray will let me do one of those moulding kits, where you can make a dildo from the mould of your penis. *Huh,* I wonder if you can add piercings to those vibrators? The more I think of it, the more appealing the idea is. There is just no way in hell I am going to ever ask Bray to do a moulding of junior for me.

Coffee, I need coffee. I need to think of coffee and not that damn pierced cucumber!

The guards at the correctional facility all know me by name. I've even become friends with one of them, Dave. He's big, buff and a total meathead, but somehow, we managed to build a little friendship. We text each other stupid cat videos. He makes me send him pictures of my dates before I go out with guys—he says it's a safety thing. I just go along with it, because he doesn't judge the volume of pictures that I've sent him over the years. He also always checks in the next morning, checking if I'm still alive, his words not mine. Dave is yet another person I haven't made mention of Bray to. Not that there is anything to mention.

"Rye Rye, you're early, babe. It's good to see you."

Dave greets me with a hug.

"You too. I have a lot going on today so I needed to come a bit earlier," I say as I start filling in the visitor information forms.

"Give me a sec. I need to organise a few more guys for the visiting room. I wasn't expecting you this early."

"Dave, you don't need any extra guards in there just because I'm here. I come every month and nothing ever happens. What do you think is going to happen?"

He raises his eyebrows at me in question, waiting me out.

"Oh please, it was one time, and that was like three years ago," I tell him defiantly.

"One time? Really, Reilly? One time, where there was a literal riot in the visiting room because one inmate made a comment about you, making the rest of them pounce on him. It took twenty guards to separate that fight. *Twenty.*"

"It wasn't that bad—you're exaggerating."

"Doesn't matter. Wait here for a minute, and stay out of trouble. I'll be back to take you through myself." He leaves me waiting at the counter as he swipes himself through the door I know leads to the visiting room. I hate this place, and I hate that my dad is stuck in this place. It's dreary and depressing. My dad needs me though. He won't admit it, but I know he looks forward to my monthly visits. Five minutes later, Dave comes back out, holding the door open and calling my name. He waits for me to enter and then follows behind me. Two steps into the room and I freeze. Something is wrong. I have that weird feeling in the pit of my stomach; one I've been getting lately whenever Bray is around. I thought I was getting sick for a while until I put it down to that pierced cucumber messing my system up.

I look around the room frantically. Dave has his hand on his taser, looking at me with concern written all across his face.

"What's wrong?" he asks as he scans the room.

I look around the room, trying to shake off the feeling, but then my eyes land on the source. I'm caught in an eye lock with Bray. I'm in shock—he is the last person I thought I would run into here. Why the hell is he here? I see he's about to stand up, but I shake my head no at him and continue walking to my dad's table. Just as I'm about to sit, Dave stops me with his hand around my arm, halting me.

"Rye, do you know Bray? And if so, how?" he whispers close to my ear.

"It's fine, Dave. I know him. I work for his brother's club. I told you about my new job."

"You forgot to mention it was at The Merge, Reilly," he accuses.

"Did I?" I shrug like it's no big deal. I totally purposefully forgot to mention I was working at The Merge. Dave has told me over and over again not to go there. Why? I don't know. But I'm guessing it has something to do with Bray being a visitor here.

"We will talk about this later," he says as he moves to the closest wall to where my dad's table is.

I sit down and finally make eye contact with my dad. "Daddy, I've missed you. How have you been?" I use my best daddy's girl voice—the one that could get me out of any trouble when I was younger.

"Don't try and sit there and daddy me, Reilly Lili." He nods his head in the direction behind me, staring daggers at the man sitting behind me. The hairs on the back of my neck are standing up, and I can feel Bray's gaze penetrating through my back.

"Care to explain to me why that guy looks like he wants to pick you up and drag you out of here, while killing every male in the room in the process?" He brings his gaze back to me and smirks, which he only does when he's trying not to laugh. What the hell? Why is he laughing at this?

"He's nobody. My friend Alyssa is dating his brother and I just started working at his brother's club."

"*Mmm*, have you told him he's a nobody?"

I nod my head. "He knows. Anyway, tell me about how you've been?" I attempt to change the subject.

"I've been good. I've missed you. How's your mum and Holly doing?" It looks like we are back to safe conversation territory. This I can handle, even with the flutters currently in my stomach.

I spend the next thirty minutes catching my father up on all the happenings from the last month. I know my time is nearly up. It always breaks my heart to leave him here.

My dad reaches across the table and grabs my hands. "Sweetheart, you can only tell yourself that someone is a nobody for so long. You can only push someone away who is willing to be lost. Do you understand?"

I nod my head, not able to form words. My dad has always been able to read me. It's like he knows my thoughts before I even know them. I don't want him to know the thoughts I've been having about Bray; I don't even want to know those thoughts.

"Reilly, that boy has not taken his eyes off you for longer than a minute the whole time you've been in the room. The only time he's not looking at you is when he's looking at every other guy in here with a direct threat in his eyes."

I shake my head no. I can feel the tears welling up in my eyes. I don't want to cry. Not here, where everyone can see me. My dad reaches up and swipes the lone, loose tear that manages to fall.

His eyes scrunching up, he questions, "Has he done something to hurt you?"

"No, it's not that. He would never hurt me, Daddy. Not intentionally anyway," I confess.

"You're scared. I get it, and I know I'm the reason why you're so afraid to open your heart." He looks down. I hate that he blames himself for my stupid hang ups.

"No, you're not. I just don't need any man in my life. I'm very content with how things are now. Why mess that up?"

He tilts his head at me. "You're content, huh? So, you wouldn't mind if Lucy over there follows that guy of yours out of here then?"

I spin my head around so fast in the direction of the Lucy he refers to that I see the blonde bombshell of a guard standing at the far wall currently eye-fucking my Bray.

Wait, hold up, he is not my anything. I shake my

head, turning back to look at my dad, who is now laughing.

"That's what I thought," he says. "You need to let go of what happened to Dylan, and the choices I made after that accident. You need to let a man into your heart, sweetheart, and whoever you choose to do that for will be the luckiest man alive. You are a beautiful person inside and out, Reilly. Any guy would be blessed to have you."

My dad looks behind me then adds, "Even if it is Brayden Johnson."

My head jerks up—Brayden Johnson is the name Bray goes by in the cage. "Wait, you know who he is?"

"Hunny, every inmate knows who he is. They stream the fights from Club M."

"So, you've seen him fight? And you still think I should give him a shot at my heart?" I ask, shocked. Bray is not the kind of guy you take home to meet your father. He's covered in ink up and down his arms. He's big, built and is as cocky as they bloody come. Yet, here my dad is, telling me to give him a fair go.

"Well, obviously he's not the first choice of guy I would choose for you, but what I see in the way he looks at you, that's why I would be okay with you dating him."

"What do you see?"

My dad thinks for a moment before saying, "I see a man who is so blindsided by love, he's willing to single-handedly take on a room full of guards and inmates for that one person. I see someone who is so besotted, he doesn't even realise it yet. I see someone who is looking at you like you're the reason the earth spins."

My mouth is hanging open; there is no way Bray has those feelings for me. He can't. We barely know each other. I think my dad has nearly lost his mind being locked up in here. "Dad, we barely even know each other. There is no way he likes me like that." Great, now I sound like a teenager.

"Reilly, I know when a man is in love and that man is very much in love with you," he persists.

"We'll have to agree to disagree then," I tell him and the moment I do, I slam my mouth shut. How the hell is that man seeping under my skin so badly that I've now taken on his stupid phrases. *Agree to disagree, my ass*. Just then, the bell rings letting me know my time is up. I stand up and hug my father, squeezing extra tight.

"I love you, Dad. See you next month."

"Love you too, sweetie. Think about what I said, please. Give my love to your mum and sister."

I nod my head. "I will."

I can't bear to see how much it hurts him when he mentions my mum and Holly. Holly comes every now and then to visit with me, but she doesn't like to. It's usually when it's been a few months and I drag her along. She loves our dad. She just hates the jail, which I get—I don't like it either.

As I make my way out, I turn back to look over my shoulder only to be greeted by a pair of green eyes.

Bray is right behind me, as he places his hand on my lower back. "Turn around and keep walking, Reilly," he grunts out.

I'm a little stunned at how close he is and by how pissed off he seems. What the hell is wrong with him? I look around the room, seeing all eyes on us. Do I have something on my face? I look over at my dad, who subtly nods his head at me and gives me his *I told you so* look.

I turn back to keep walking towards the door. Dave is standing in the doorway with his arms folded over his chest. He does not look happy either. I don't know what it is with all the men in this place, but I need to get out of here and away from all of their moody asses.

"Dave, it's been a pleasure as always," I say to him as I get to the door. He doesn't answer, and instead he looks over my shoulder at Bray.

"I'm going to have to ask you to remove your hands off the lady," Dave asserts to Bray. I can feel Bray's body vibrating behind me, and I hear him growl. Shit, I have to do something to put this fire out, before he can do something stupid like start a brawl in the lockup with a guard, which for sure would see him in this exact same lock up.

I step forward putting a slight space between Bray and me, only he steps forward with me. Damn him and his macho shit. Fine, another tactic. I step to the side and take hold of his hand. I wait for shock to cross his face at me holding his hand but get nothing. He is stoic.

Holding his hand is strangely comforting but I don't have time to deal with those feelings right now.

"Dave, have you met my boyfriend—Bray?" I ask with a huge fake-ass smile plastered across my face.

"Your boyfriend? Really, Reilly? That's what you're going with?" Dave asks me while shaking his head.

"Yes, Dave, boyfriend. Now kindly open the door so I can get on with my day."

"Whatever you say, princess," Dave replies as he opens the door. I feel Bray try to slip his hand free. *Ahh, no way, mate, not today.* I give him my best glare and pull him out behind me. I don't stop to say goodbye to the ladies at the counter, like I usually do. I head straight for the door and wait for them to buzz us out. I don't let go of Bray's hand as I lead him through the carpark right up to my car.

# CHAPTER EIGHT

BRAY

*I*'M SITTING in the visiting room of Silverwater Correctional Facility visiting my mate Dan. He's been here for five months now for some petty assault; he beat the shit out of someone who fucking deserved it. The government should be thanking him, not putting him behind bars. I visit as much as I can, which some months is not very often, considering we've been mates since grade school. Although my visit now is more business than pleasure.

I'm here to put an end to the fucker who thought they could mess with Alyssa. Even if it was two years ago and she wasn't part of my family then, she is now. Which means the fucktard that stalked and attacked her has to go. I finish telling Dan about what I need done. I talk in code using my fights as a key, because that's something we have in common—Dan has never missed a fight of mine.

"Remember that fight between me and the guy who called himself stalk attack?" I ask him, folding the sleeves of my shirt up.

"Yeah, fucker never saw you coming," he replies.

I nod my head while scratching at my arm, where I just happen to have the inmate number scrawled into the design of a tattoo. "Yeah, good times, can't wait for a replay," I tell him.

I watch as he stares at the numbers that he knows are not permanently there. Dan nods his head and leans back in his chair.

"How's the family?" he asks.

"Good, Zac's practically married up to this chick Alyssa he met a hot minute ago. Ella's getting ready to go off to uni next year."

"Fuck, man, Zac bit the bullet, hey? Never thought I'd see the day."

"Yeah, me either. But he's totally gone. Good girl too, way too good for the likes of that grouchy bastard, but what can you do." I shrug my shoulders.

It's good to talk shit with Dan again. I've missed this, the easiness that has always been between us. I look around and notice a shit ton more guards in the room than normal.

"What's with the extra meat?" I ask.

Dan looks around, spots an older guy sitting at a

table and turns back to me. "The guy's daughter comes in once a month. Always the first Sunday of the month. Sometimes there's two of them but mostly just the one. They always put extra guards in the room whenever she visits," he says.

"Are they famous or something? That seems extreme for one chick."

"Not famous, but his daughters are smoking hot, both of them obviously—they look the fucking same."

Just then, the hairs on my arms stand up. Something is not right. I look towards the door where someone has just walked in. "Fuck, what the actual fuck?" I say loud enough for only Dan to hear me. He turns and spots her.

"Yep, that's her. Told you she's fucking smoking hot." He smirks at me.

I give him a death glare. "Watch your fucking mouth, never speak about her like that again."

"*Woah*, mate, what the hell? Hang on, do you know her?"

I don't answer. I can't take my eyes off her. The fact that the guard who walked her in seems way too familiar with her is pissing me the fuck off. Something is wrong—why is she looking around the room like she's searching for something? The moment her eyes connect with mine, she stops, shock showing on her face.

The douche next to her reaches out and touches her arm before asking her something. I'm about to get up out of my chair and drag her back out the door she came through. I stop though, when she subtly shakes her head no at me and continues walking over to what I now know is her dad's table.

Fuck me, this is no place for a girl like her to be visiting. I understand the extra guards in the room now. As I look around, every fucking male has their eyes glued to her. I want to ring the necks of each and every single one of them. I'm making a point to them as best I can when I catch their attention; once they notice I'm giving them the look of the reaper, they avert their eyes.

"Who bit that bullet?" Dan asks me.

"I have fucking bit no bullet, idiot," I deny.

"Are you sure about that? Because you haven't heard a word that I've said for the last ten minutes, and you haven't taken your eyes off that girl for longer than one."

"She's one of Alyssa's best friends. She also works at the club, so I'm just looking out for her, that's all."

"Deny it all you like. I know you better than you know yourself. You, my friend, are head over heels in love with that girl." Dan smirks.

"Fuck. Okay, I like her, junior likes her even more, but she won't give me the time of day. Stop laughing, fucker. We've never had this issue before. You know as well as I do—the ladies have never refused a playdate with junior before." I shrug like it's not a big deal.

"First, stop talking to me about your dick—never

talk to me about your fucking dick. Second, stop crying like a little bitch. I never thought I'd see the day Bray Johnson forfeits a fight," Dan laughs. "You're a fighter, Bray. Fight for the girl you're in love with."

He's right. I do need to fight harder to get Reilly to realise that she's mine. "You're right. I'm not giving up, just formulating my fight plan."

"Do me a favour and wait to have the wedding until I'm out of this joint, because that's bound to be one hell of a bachelor party and I want in on that shit," Dan laughs. I ignore him and continue to watch Reilly with her dad, who is occasionally glaring back at me.

"What's he in here for?" I ask Dan.

"Who?" he asks looking around. "Oh, your girl's dad?"

"Yeah."

"Heard his son was killed by a drunk driver. The justice system let the driver off, so the dude went and shot him close range."

What the actual fuck? Reilly had a brother who was killed and her dad landed himself in jail. Well, her resistance to getting too close to men is making sense now. The way she closed herself off that morning the cops showed up on my door, it all makes sense. Fuck, I'm an idiot. Why didn't I just tell her why I got arrested? She probably thinks the worst possible scenarios. How could she not?

I watch as her dad lifts his hand to her; it looks like he's swiping a tear from her face. Why the hell is she crying? It takes everything in me not to get up and go to her. It should be me offering her comfort right now; it should be me wiping the tears away from her face.

I wait until the bell rings and I see her start to stand. "Good chat, mate. Gotta go. See you next time," I say to Dan as I stand and walk towards Reilly.

I LET Reilly tug me out of the jail, as much as I wanted to pummel the guard who told me not to touch her. Not to touch? He had the nerve to tell me I couldn't touch what's mine. Fuck him. My girl put him straight anyway. Just don't tell her she's my girl, because she'd run a mile.

As soon as we make it to her car, I spin her around, pinning her back to the door. I don't waste time or give her any time for thought as I slam my lips against hers. The moment my lips make contact, I feel like I've just come home, her touch sending bolts of lightning through my whole body.

I've kissed a lot of women, too many to count. But no one has ever made me feel the way kissing Reilly makes me feel. It's at this moment that I consider that Dan might be right. I could actually love this girl. Fuck, now I sound like I've lost my balls.

Pressing into Reilly harder, I make sure she can feel just how happy junior is with this kiss. He's as hard as a fucking rock. Reilly groans into my mouth and pulls on my neck, tugging me even closer if that's possible. We duel for control of the kiss but there's no way I'm giving up control right now. I could fight with our tongues like this forever and not get bored. She growls and I can't help but laugh a little.

Pulling back, I smirk at her as she pushes against my chest. I see the moment that she recognises what she just did. "What the hell, Bray? You can't just kiss me like that whenever you damn well feel like it!" she yells.

"Why not? You didn't seem to be complaining a minute ago, babe." Raising my eyebrows at her, I give her the best panty-melting smirk I can muster.

"Shut up, and stop looking at me like that. It's not fair." She stomps and pouts. Literally pouts, and it's cute as hell.

"Sugar, you told that douche back there that I was your boyfriend. I've never really had a girlfriend before, but I'm pretty sure the title gives me permission to kiss *my girlfriend* whenever and wherever I want. What kind of boyfriend would I be if I left you hanging?"

I watch the redness creep up her pale skin, starting at the top of her breasts and running all the way up her neck and face. She's blushing—I actually managed to get her to blush. Point one for team Bray, zero for team Reilly.

"Well, first, he's not a douche; he happens to be one of my good friends. Second, you and I both know you are most certainly not my damn boyfriend, Bray."

"We'll agree to disagree on that fact until you catch up, because you are mine, Reilly. I'm not about to give up on you. You want to run? That's fine. I'll chase. You want to hide? No worries. I'll hunt. You want to live in denial and tell everyone that you're not mine? I'll buy a fucking skywriter, announcing the fusion of Brielly to the whole of Sydney."

"Has anyone ever told you that you're bloody looney, Bray? And what the hell is the fusion of Brielly?" she asks.

I reach out and pull her body tight against mine, hugging her in a tight hug. At first, she's stiff, but then she softens and leans in, wrapping her arms around my waist. I wait like this for a moment, enjoying the feel of her in my arms. This is what we should be doing, not arguing about me being her boyfriend.

I kiss her forehead and pull back a little to look down at her face, tucking her hair behind her ear so I get an uninterrupted view of the beauty that is Reilly.

"I'm glad you asked. The fusion of Brielly is you and me, babe, Bray and Reilly fused together. Now, there will be hearts broken all over Sydney once all the ladies read that announcement, and all of their broken and shattered dreams will land on my shoulders. But for you, I'm willing to take that burden."

Reilly laughs a little before she catches herself. "If there are so many ladies out there with their sights set on you, what on earth do you want with me?"

"Well, there may be a bunch of other women out there I could have—and you and I both know that's true—let's not try to deny my hotness factor, babe," I say, waving my hand down my body. I don't mind making a fool of myself if it brings a smile to her face, which it does. "There is, however, only one of you. You are the one who I want and I always get what I want. No matter how hard the fight is, I will win."

"Actually, there are two of me!" she exclaims.

"*Uhh,* no, you and Holly may look alike, but you are different people. You are one of a kind, Reilly. I see it—everyone around you sees it. I will make it my mission to make you see it too."

"It doesn't matter. I have things to do, people to see. Thanks for yet again a memorable kiss." She turns and unlocks her car.

"I'll follow you out. I'm just parked across there," I say pointing to my car. I open her door and wait for her to get in before shutting it and walking to my own car.

Why do I have the feeling that she just shut me down? Whatever she tries to tell me and herself, I know she feels something. You don't kiss like that if you don't feel it.

I start my car, pull out, drive around, and pull up behind her car; she hasn't left her spot yet. I wait a moment and then jump out and head to her window. I hear her car try to start over but it's not going. I tap her window and step back and wait for her to get out.

"Need help?" I ask.

"I don't know what happened. This has never happened to her before. I think she's sick or something, Bray." She looks at the car with concern. I laugh a little because it's fucking funny how she talks about her car.

Pulling out my phone, I fire off a text to a guy I know at a garage not too far from here. I get a response immediately, saying he will come and get her car. "I know a guy. He's coming to get your car and tow it back to his shop. I'm sure he'll have it up and running by tomorrow," I reassure her.

"Lock your car, and we'll drop the keys off to the garage for him on the way back."

"Okay, thank you," she agrees as she locks her car and walks to the passenger side of mine. I run to catch up with her, her easy agreement catching me off guard a little. I open her door and wait for her to get in before shutting it and making my way to the driver's side.

# CHAPTER NINE

REILLY

ITTING in the passenger side of Bray's car is unnerving. I can smell him everywhere. He's so close I could easily reach over and touch him. Boy, do I want to touch him, all over. I want to slide my hands, my tongue, all over the grooves of his body.

As much as I want to touch him, kiss him and do much more dirtier things to him and with him, I can't. At least not right now. I need to figure out how I am going to get to the cemetery to visit with Dylan. I could get an Uber after I get Bray to drop me home, but that will not leave me with any time to get ready for that stupid double date tonight.

Bray reaches over and grabs hold of my hand. Momentarily, I consider shaking his hold off and removing my hand from his. As I'm staring down at our joined hands, contemplating the mixed feelings I am fighting at the moment, Bray's voice breaks through my fog.

"Babe, I can hear you thinking. What's wrong?" he questions. How is he so intuitive to my mind? I'm leaning more and more towards some kind of witchery shit going on. I've never met a guy who can read me so well, other than my dad.

I debate what to tell him. Can I ask him to drop me at the cemetery? Then I will have to answer all the usual questions and tell him about Dylan. I'm not sure I'm ready for that conversation. The other option is pulling out of this double date with Holly and letting her down, which I just can't do. She hardly ever dates so it's a big deal for her to put herself out there, even if I think the guy is a douchebag. I don't have to like him.

"Do you think you can drop me at the cemetery? I have to do something there. I'll get Holly to come and pick me up from there." I ask him so fast that I don't even know if it's possible to understand the gibberish that just came out of my mouth.

He squeezes my hand; it's so comforting and reassuring and foreign. I should not be comforted by him. I should not want to be comforted by him, yet I do.

"Sure, which cemetery do you need to go to?" he asks. "Uh, the Rockwood one?" Why that came out as a question, I have no freaking idea. "Are you sure?" he asks.

"Yep, I'm sure. The Rockwood. Thank you." "No problem." He leaves it at that.

I don't get it. Where is the barrage of questions? The *why do you want to go there?* And the *who died?* Or the usual awkward silences and the *I'm sorry* when people find out I had a brother who died way too young.

But Bray didn't even show any kind of emotion or questioning when I asked about going to the cemetery. It's as if I asked him to drive through McDonald's for a Big Mac.

"Why are you not asking questions about why I'm going to the cemetery?" I blurt out. Way to play it cool, Reilly.

Bray looks over and seems to study my face for what feels like forever.

"Do you want me to question you about it?"

"No, I don't. It's just weird. Most people ask me why I visit the cemetery." I try to explain my weirdness.

"Well, I'm not most people, babe. You and I both know I'm better than the rest." He winks at me.

I laugh. I love that he can make me feel that little bit less awkward and self-conscious by just being his usual silly self. I know he does it on purpose—there is a lot more depth to Bray than the pretty face and cocky attitude he lets everyone else see.

"Look, if you want to talk about it, I'm all ears. If not, I'll wait until you do," he tells me, and a heap more bricks tumble to the ground from around my heart. Damn him and his near perfectness.

BRAY TURNS the car off after pulling into the cemetery. He jumps out and walks around to my door, opening it before I even get my bearings together.

"Thanks for the lift. I appreciate it. I guess I'll see you tonight?" I ask.

"Babe, if you think for a second, I'm leaving you here you're crazier than Harley Quinn. You go do what you have to do. I'll wait here," he says as he leans against his car.

"You don't need to do that. Holly will come and get me. It's fine," I argue.

"I know I don't have to, but I want to. I'm not leaving, even if you call Holly. I will be waiting right here for you, Reilly."

Man, he is persistent. I don't even know how to argue with that. "Well, it's just I don't know how long I will be," I tell him honestly; I have a lot to fill Dylan in on from the past month.

"Doesn't matter, take your time. I have some emails and calls to make anyway." He leans in and kisses me gently on the lips, sealing the deal. Okay, I guess he's waiting for me.

I spend a bit of time pulling out weeds that have grown around Dylan's headstone since my last visit. Then I make myself comfortable and sit, leaning up against the headstone, and tell my brother all about what's been happening.

I tell him about Alyssa meeting Zac, I tell him about my new job, about Mum and Holly, and about the visit I just had with Dad. I know I've been sitting here a while but there is one more person I need to tell him about. I lean back and close my eyes; I can see his face when I close my eyes.

*I think I met someone, Dyl. You'd like him, I'm sure. His name's Bray, and he's hot, smoking hot. Not that you want to know that. I don't know how to let him in though. I'm struggling. I want to let him in. I want to say fuck it and let go of all my baggage and issues and give this thing with him a red-hot go. I'm just scared. I'm so fucking scared, Dylan.*

*I'm scared of the possibilities, of him being taken away just like you and Daddy were. I'm scared that I'll end up more invested than he is. I'm scared he will wake up and see how messed up I am and how much better than me he can do. What if I let go and let him into my heart, only for him to crush it? I don't know if I can take that chance of being hurt like that.*

*I'm not strong like Mum and Holly. Dad thinks I should give him a shot. Can you believe that? Dad. Our dad knows Bray is an underground cage fighter and he told me to give the guy a chance. It's very possible Dad's reaching that age we used to joke about, where he starts to lose his mind.*

*I wish you were here to tell me what to do. I could really use your wisdom right now; you always were the smarter and wiser sibling. I haven't told Mum or Holly about how I'm feeling, although Holly probably knows—she always bloody knows.*

*What the hell do I do, Dylan? I need you to give me a sign or something. Is this the person I'm meant to let break down my walls? Because it might be too late if he's not; those walls are crumbling down faster than I can rebuild them.*

I open my eyes and sit up straighter. My eyes land on the man in question. He's still standing, leaning against his car and staring straight at me. Great, he probably thinks I'm fucking looney for sure now. He's just watched me talk to myself for the last thirty minutes. He's still there though, that has to mean something. I look up to the sky. *Please tell me this is your sign, Dylan*, I whisper before standing and dusting off my dress.

I make my way back to the car, back to Bray. He doesn't take his eyes off me. As soon as I reach him, he grabs me and pulls me in tight. His hugs are something else. I can't help but melt into him, returning his hug. I wrap my arms around his waist and bury my head into his chest. I let myself have this moment; I embrace the comfort that he offers me in this hug.

Bray runs his hands through my hair and kisses me on the forehead. Why does that feel so nice? It's odd, almost nurturing. But I'll take it.

"You good?" he asks as he pulls back from our hug.

*Well, I was good when your arms were wrapped around me,* I think to myself. No way in hell I'm telling him that though. Instead, I nod my head, not trusting myself to speak.

"Let's go then. I'm going to stop by my place and shower real quick then take you to yours. I'll wait while you get ready for our hot date tonight." He waggles his eyebrows up and down.

"Not a hot date. I was roped into this, remember. Also, don't let your expectations of how fun it will be tonight run wild. You have not met Holly's date and trust me, double dating with Holl is usually anything but fun," I warn him.

"Well, it'll be fun because I'll be going on my first official date with my new hot as fuck girlfriend." Bray smirks.

"Not a date and still not your girlfriend, Bray," I inform him.

"Sure you are, you just don't want to say it out loud yet." He's so bloody confident, although if I looked like him, I probably would be too. I can't help but smile at him. "You should make it easier on yourself and just admit it already. It's fate, babe. Brielly is happening."

"I'm not sure I believe in fate. I think people make their own paths in life by their own choices." I'm almost one hundred percent certain I don't believe in fate.

"Well, damn, babe, way to be a pessimist. Don't you worry your pretty little head though. I've got enough faith in our *fate* for the both of us."

Why did my heart have to go and get all mushy over this guy? Why not just a quiet guy who didn't challenge me? *Because you'd be bored as hell, Reilly*, that little devil in my head tells me. She's right I would be bored. Also, Bray sure is real pretty to look at.

I look him up and down. The man is fine; it's unfair how bloody good looking those family genes are. His strong chiselled jaw, those green eyes that draw me in and hold me captivated, and don't even get me started on his body.

As perfect as his exterior package is, it's what's on the inside that I'm in trouble of getting attached to. His damn personality is making me want to give in and give this steady relationship thing a go.

He seems genuine—his actions speak louder than any words. As I look at him, I consider everything he has shown me, all the little ways he shows he cares. The way he waited silently at the cemetery, not pushing me for information, that shows me that he wants to give me the time I need to open up to him.

Do I need more time though? I'm certainly not ready to tell him all about Dylan or my dad. I don't need to see the sympathetic look in his eyes. But I could be ready to give him a chance, to give us a chance.

As much as I don't want to admit it, he's already cracked his way through my defences, seeped into my bloodstream. I can't get him out of my head. When I'm with him, I feel comfortable; I feel safe and I feel like I'm at home, where I'm meant to be. All of these feelings scare the shit out of me and make me want to run a mile.

I consider what my dad said to me, how he encouraged me to give love a shot. Maybe it won't end in tragedy. Maybe even if it does, the time we have together now will make it worth it. At least that's what my mum tells me. The years she had with my dad were the best of her life, and the years she will continue to have with him when he gets out of jail will continue to be her best years.

Taking a deep breath in, I quickly confess before I lose my bravery, "Okay, maybe I like you a little bit." The biggest smile spreads across his face.

"But, I don't know how this can work. I work for your brother, Bray. I don't want to lose my job when you decide that I'm not good enough for you. I also don't want to make it awkward for Alyssa and Zac when we don't work out." I tell him all of my fears and reasons we should not be together.

"First, Zac would not fire you because of me. Trust me, he does not make emotional decisions relating to the club. Well, at least he didn't before he met Alyssa. Secondly, you're not good enough for me? You're too damn good for the likes of me and you can most certainly do better, but I don't care. I'm selfish and I'm keeping you anyway." He gives me a look, daring me to challenge him on that.

This is happening all too fast; I don't know how to handle this. I want to take my dad's advice and give this thing a shot. I'm just not sure I'm prepared for the potential loss or hurt that will come from this fusion as Bray calls it. Then I come up with an idea, a trial before you buy kind of thing.

"Maybe we can give this a go and see what happens with us, but it has to stay between us. I don't want any of our friends or family knowing that we are dating yet."

"You want to sneak around like kids—maybe play seven minutes in heaven too?"

"Well, I can always go back to pretending you don't exist?" I tease, like that would ever be possible.

"Harsh, babe! I didn't say I didn't want to sneak around with you. If that's what you want to do, then that's what we'll do. For now." He looks over and smiles at me. "Besides, from what I remember, seven minutes in heaven was a fun game."

"Don't insult junior. You and I both know he's going to need more than seven minutes." Wait, why on earth am I referring to his dick as junior too? I swear this man is rubbing off on me too much.

BRAY WAS super quick to shower and get ready. I made sure to stay out in his living room while he was in the shower, otherwise we would probably still be in there. Looking down at my phone, I wonder if we have time to shower together at my house, because the idea of showering with Bray—with his wet and nakedness all on display for me to touch and lick—yeah, that is very appealing.

We pull into my driveway and I groan. Can anything go my way today?

"What's wrong?" Bray asks.

"Okay, listen. I know Holly and I are way too old to be living at home with our mum, but we do, so you just have to deal with that."

He laughs, like full-on belly laughs at me. "It's not funny, Bray. You haven't met my mum. I thought she'd still be at work, but apparently the universe hates me today and she's home. If you want to wait here in the car, I understand. You do not have to come inside and endure the craziness that is my family."

"Babe, if your mum is anywhere near as feisty as you or as sweet as Holly, I will love her. Besides, women love me! I've never had an issue getting one not to." He winks.

Cocky fucking bastard. Well, let's just see how much he loves the attention of Lynne Reynolds, aka my mother. She has not had a male to fuss over in a very long time. Holly and I never bring dates home, so the fact that Bray is here now is a bigger deal than he knows.

"Okay, but don't say I didn't warn you," I tell him as I get out of the car.

I'm just around the hood of the car when I'm met with a sour-faced Bray. "What on earth crawled up your ass in the last five seconds to create that look?" I ask him. I swear the guy is more hormonal than a nine-month pregnant chick.

"You didn't wait for me to open your door." He pouts, like full on bottom lip out pouts. It's so freaking cute it's ridiculous.

"Get used to it, baby. I'm not waiting around for doors to be opened for me. I open them myself. I'm a grown-ass woman like that," I declare as I march towards the house. I need to set him straight from the get-go. I am not a wilting flower who will let his alpha ass come and control everything.

Before I can open the front door, Bray reaches out and grabs me around my waist. He spins me and has my back pinned against the door so fast I lose my balance. The only thing holding me upright is the grip of Bray's arms around my waist. The next second, his lips are on mine, his tongue swiping the seams while seeking entrance.

Entrance that I greedily grant him. I moan into his mouth, electric shocks raging a war through my body. I need more than just this kiss; I need it all. Grabbing onto his neck, I jump, wrapping my legs around his waist. His hands move to my butt, caressing as he pushes me into the door harder.

Now, this is what I need. I grind my core onto him. I can feel his cock, hard and ready to play. I recall just how good at play it was too.

"You have no idea how much I fucking like you," Bray whispers in my ear as he kisses his way down my neck. "Everything about you is fucking perfect, Reilly. I love that you're strong and independent, loyal and feisty as fuck." He continues kissing and nipping at my ear, while I continue to dry hump him like a dog in heat. "But, no matter how capable you are, I will always open doors for you, Reilly. Not because you can't do it, because I know you can do fucking anything. I'll open them because I want to, because you deserve to be treated like the queen you are and I'd be a pretty shitty boyfriend if I failed at doing that."

More kisses, then he bites down hard on my neck. "*Ahh*, God. That. Yes. Keep doing that," I demand. I'm so close to coming, my core is grinding onto him, and my lace panties are soaked through. Oh God, I'm probably leaving wet marks all over the front of his jeans. I don't care right now though.

Bray chuckles as he continues his torture to my body. "You know, you're the best girlfriend I've ever had, Reilly," he declares.

"I'm the only girlfriend you've ever had, idiot."

"Yeah, but you're still the best," he says as his lips return to mine. I need to move this party inside, preferably to my bed, or shower—either one is fine with me.

Oh God, this kiss is something else. I feel the wall behind me fall away, and the next minute, I'm floating. Bray pulls back, and his hold around my back tightens as he clears his throat.

"*Arghh*, why'd you stop?" I am not impressed with the change of events.

"*Ahh*, that'd probably be for my benefit, Reilly Lili."

Oh shit, my eyes widen at Bray. I've just been caught making out at the front door like a teenager by my mum. "Shit, fuck, shit," I curse my luck as I untangle myself from Bray and get my feet back on the ground.

# CHAPTER TEN

*Bray*

*W*ELL, this is not awkward at all. Reilly climbs down and lands on her feet in front of me. Turning, she goes to step to the side, but I take hold of her hips, keeping her in place. Right in front of me. There are some things that her mother should never see, my hard-on being one of them.

Reilly looks back at me over her shoulder and smirks. She knows exactly why I don't want her to move just yet. We need to get junior under control first. Reaching my hand out around Reilly, I hold it out to her mum.

"Hi, Mrs. Reynolds, I'm Bray. It's nice to meet you." I wait for her to shake my hand. She pushes Reilly aside, squeezing her way between us and hugs me.

"There's no need for such formalities. You can call me Lynne. Welcome," she says as she steps back. "Come in, come in," she continues as she grabs my hand and pulls me through the door. I look at Reilly, who is just staring at me with an *I told you so* face.

At least junior recognised the mum hug and retreated really quickly, saving me from a very embarrassing and uncomfortable moment. It's been a long time since I've had a mum hug, a really fucking long time, and Reilly's mum just hugged me like she's known me my whole life. I wouldn't say no to one of those again—I was very much a mumma's boy growing up.

Zac was always stoic and quiet for as long as I can remember and Ella was the apple of everyone's eye, daddy's little girl, the family princess. Not much has changed there. She's still the family princess.

I let Lynne pull me through the house. It's a nice family home. As I'm dragged through the hallways, I can see tons of pictures on the walls. They are mostly of the twins and who I assume is their brother. I pass pictures where I can't make out which twin is which. We end up in the kitchen where Lynne deposits me at the counter.

"Sit down, love. Now, Reilly didn't tell me she was bringing anyone home, so you will have to excuse the mess and my unpreparedness."

I look around the pristine kitchen, and there is not

a thing out of place. It's a large kitchen with oak doors and white bench-tops, and stainless steel appliances. I seek out Reilly because I honestly am at a loss for words. For once in my life, I don't know what to say. Why the fuck am I so nervous? My leg starts jittering under the counter. I get antsy when I get nervous, which is rarely ever. I'd usually just head to the gym and hit something when I feel like this, but that is not a possibility here.

As my gaze connects with Reilly's, something inside me settles. It's odd because I usually need to fight, run, or work out until I collapse when I get jittery like this. For some kind of calmness to come over me just because I've locked eyes with her makes me think I might have had one too many hits to the head, and they are finally catching up with me.

"Mum, we aren't staying. I'm just going to go change and then we're going out with Holly," she explains.

"Oh, nonsense, Reilly. You go get ready. I'll look after your friend here." Her mum waves her off.

"Do not make him food, Mum. We don't want him getting too comfortable here," Reilly says as she turns and walks out of the kitchen, leaving me alone with her mum. That's brave of her. If she thinks I'm not going to pull out all the charm to win her mother over, she clearly does not know me very well.

"What would you like to drink, love? I've got soft drinks, coffee, tea? I don't have any beer, sorry. If I'd known you were coming, I would have catered better for your visit."

"Oh, you don't need to cater for me, Lynne. I'll have a water if it's not too much trouble," I say, giving her my full smile, dimples and all.

"Of course." She busies herself filling a glass with ice and then water from the refrigerator. She places the cup down in front of me and then returns to the fridge, pulling out some sort of cake slice looking deliciousness.

"I don't have much, but I made this fresh this morning, chocolate mint slice. Here, try some," she says as she shoves a huge slice in front of me.

Normally, I would not go for this type of treat; I'm very careful about what I put into my body. But I don't have another fight for a few weeks now—I can afford to let myself go a little.

I take a huge forkful of the slice and moan. "Oh my God, this is good, Lynne. Really fucking good," I say around another mouthful of slice.

I then take note that I just cursed in front of Reilly's mum on the first visit here. "Shit, sorry, I didn't mean to curse. It's just really good slice," I say, hoping she won't hold it against me.

Lynne laughs, "Do not sensor yourself for me, love. I've been around longer than you. There is nothing you can say that will shock me, trust me."

I smile as I take another bite of the slice. I could really get used to this kind of catering. "Can Reilly cook like this? Because if so, I might just have to whisk her off to Vegas tonight and marry her," I confess. The idea sounds appealing—I'd like to see her try to run and hide once I get a ring on her finger.

Where the fuck are these thoughts coming from? I have no idea. Fucking hits to the head, they must be catching up. Or maybe it's sappy Zac rubbing off on me. His happy and in love, nothing can bring him down attitude is enough to rub off on the grinch.

"You might want to hold off that proposal, Romeo.

Reilly doesn't cook or bake." Lynne laughs. "That's a shame," I pout.

"So, you and Reilly. How long has that been happening?" she questions. I'm surprised it took this long for her to bring out the questions.

DRIVING to the restaurant with Reilly next to me is painful. I have to mentally remind myself to keep my eyes on the road. She's wearing a black dress, or the hankie she is passing off as a fucking dress. It's high up on her chest—there is no cleavage showing whatsoever —but that does not distract from her impressive rack being on full display, the material hugging and caressing her breasts just like my hands are itching to do.

The dress is short—her long, lean legs on display. And then there's the shoes. I can't wait for dinner to be over so I can take her home and have her in nothing but those fucking stilettos.

My hand rests on her thigh, my fingers absently stroking up and down the smooth skin. Skin I want to lick, suck, and bite all over. Her skin pebbles with goosebumps under my fingers. I don't miss her slight squirm and the way she squeezes her thighs together.

"You cold, babe?" I ask her.

She glares at me. "You know damn well I'm not bloody cold. I'm horny, Bray—so freaking horny that if you don't pull this car over and help a girl out, I am going to excuse myself to the bathroom when we get to this restaurant and help myself."

I don't know if she is serious or not right now, but I'm not taking the chance. I find a side road and turn down it, pulling the car over. I don't say anything.

I unclip my seatbelt then lean across and unclip hers. I'm silent as my hand slides up her legs; she's not shy as she spreads her legs as wide as she can in her seat. My hand slides up under her dress and I'm shocked when I'm met with bare skin.

"Fuck, Reilly, you're not wearing panties," I groan out. "*Mmm*, I didn't want panty lines in my dress."

That's her answer, she didn't want fucking panty lines.

"How do you expect me to sit through dinner, knowing you're bare under this dress? To know that my dessert is ready and waiting for me?"

I slam two fingers into her warm, wet pussy. My mouth salivates. I can remember the taste of her on my tongue. Reilly arches off the seat, pushing herself against my hand. I use my thumb to circle her clit while pumping in and out of her. Her moans fill the car; her scent surrounds me. My cock is fucking hard; junior wants to come out and join the party.

"I can smell you. I can feel how warm and wet your pussy is for me. The way it's strangling my fingers, I can't wait to feel this pussy strangle my cock again."

She responds to my words so well, moving her pelvis in time with my fingers pumping. She grinds down on my thumb that continues its slow torturous circles around her clit.

"I'm going to bury my cock so far inside this pussy, you

won't know where I end and you begin; we will be fused together. Do you want that? Do you want my cock inside this hungry little pussy of yours?" I don't expect her to answer but she does.

"Now, I want it now, Bray."

"Demanding little thing when you're horny, aren't you? You can't have my cock now. You're going to come on my hand now, Reilly. Then you will sit through the whole of dinner knowing that by the end of the night, my cock will be buried deep inside your cunt."

"*Argh*, why can't I have it now? I need it," she argues. She's so close to coming though. I can feel her body quaking, trembling all over, the urgency in her movements increasing.

"Be a good girl, Reilly, and come for me now," I demand, my voice husky and filled with need. She does not let me down. She comes all over my fingers, her screams of pleasure music to my fucking ears. I ease up my strokes as she comes down from her orgasmic bliss.

Her cheeks are rosy and her face a picture of pure bliss and relaxation. I ease my fingers out of her, putting them straight to my mouth. Now it's my turn to moan. Her taste is just as fucking sweet and delicious as I remember. I take my time licking all of her juices off my fingers, savouring the taste.

"Thank you," I say to her as I gently kiss her lips. "You're welcome?" she questions.

I can't help but laugh as I pull the seatbelt over her and buckle her back in. "Let's hope this dinner goes fast so I can get you home and naked in my bed."

As I'm buckling my seatbelt, Reilly halts my movement, grabbing my arm. "Wait, don't you want me to, you know, return the favour?" she asks, waving her hand in the direction of my very obvious cock.

"As much as I would love that, the next time I come is going to be when my cock is buried inside your pussy," I declare.

"*Ahh*, okay then." She lets go of my arm and settles into the seat. "You're really good at that, by the way."

I laugh. "What kind of boyfriend would I be if I wasn't? I can't have my girlfriend left unsatisfied and wanting, now can I? That would not be good for my rep."

"Don't you think you're wearing out that whole boyfriend/girlfriend title thing already?" She smiles.

"Probably, we should go to Vegas and get married by Elvis, then I can move on to calling you my wife already. Also, I look fucking great in a tux." My suggestion is not received well.

"Please tell me you are joking and haven't gone all grade-A crazy on me already. I'm barely accepting that you have the boyfriend label, Bray. There is no way in hell you're getting promoted to husband label after one day of actual dating. Who does that anyway? That's crazy. Like straight jacket kind of crazy. Should I call Zac now and tell him he needs to have you scheduled? Are you sick?" She finishes her rambling with the back of her hand against my forehead.

"Not sick, babe. Relax, it was a joke." I watch as her

body begins to relax before I tack on the "mostly" to the end of my sentence. She glares at me. I think I need to remind myself that this one is a flight risk; I need to think before I speak a bit more. It was a joke though; I couldn't actually fly her to Vegas to marry her tonight. I wouldn't be able to get a jet booked until at least tomorrow.

# CHAPTER ELEVEN

REILLY

*T*HIS DINNER IS the worst double date I have ever been on with Holly. I've been sitting here bored out of my mind, listening to her date drone on and on about being a sports teacher. Newsflash, my twin sister is a freaking teacher. I don't need a play by play on your job, mate.

I'm also waiting for Bray to reach his boiling point. I can tell he's holding back. I've seen the death glare he's been giving the guy each time his eyes spend way too much time on my breasts. Why? I have no idea. Holly's are literally identical—we have the same size and shape breasts.

His leering creeps me out majorly, but I try not to let it show. I'm trying to distract Bray from the fact that he wants to reach across the table and ring this dude's neck. At least that's the vibes I'm getting from him. By the looks Holly keeps shooting me, she is getting the same vibes.

I slide my hand up his thigh. I'm beginning to come around to this whole boyfriend/girlfriend thing more and more. If Bray's my boyfriend, that means I get to touch him as much as I want, wherever I want, and that is very appealing. To have twenty-four hours, seven days a week access to his body, a girl could only be so lucky. Oh, wait! I'm that girl. I'm that lucky, *huh*.

My hand continues to travel up his thigh until I reach the inner most upper part of his thigh. He shifts in his seat. My hand continues its slow pursuit of junior. I finally reach my target and rub my hand over his crotch. I keep my touch light, almost featherlight. I can feel his cock harden under my fingers.

Bray leans in and whispers in my ear, "You're playing with fire, baby."

I smile back at him, challenging him to bring whatever he has. At least my distraction technique has worked. He is not looking like he's ready to jump the table just yet.

I pick up my glass of wine with my free hand and gulp a mouthful. Before I can even swallow, Bray's fingers slam inside me. And the suddenness of the intrusion makes me choke. Wine comes spitting out of my mouth, projecting all the way across the table and landing across the front of the shirt Holly's date is wearing.

I'm still recovering, Bray's fingers still buried in my pussy, when Holly's date pushes his chair back and jumps up. "What the fuck? Are you a fucking idiot?" he yells in my direction.

Just as fast as those fingers were inside me, they were ripped out, as Bray jumps over the table. Like literally freaking ninja jumps over the table. It all happens so fast. I haven't even recovered from my choking episode and Bray has Holly's date by the throat.

I can see his body vibrating from here. Holly moves around the table to my side; she does not do well with confrontation or violence.

"Who the fuck do you think you're talking to like that, fucker?" Bray growls into his face. He doesn't give him time to answer, if he could come up with an answer. The guy's motionless, frozen like a deer caught in headlights.

"I'll tell you who, my fucking girlfriend, my queen, that's who. Nobody talks to her like that and goes unscathed."

Holly's eyes widen as she mouths the words to me. *Girlfriend? Queen?* I shrug in answer because honestly, how does one respond to that? I think this boyfriend label has definitely gone to his ego-induced head.

"*Ahh*, baby, you need to tone it down a notch." I put on my sugary sweet voice and walk around the table.

It's nice that Bray was quick to stick up for me, but I've been sticking up for myself for a very long time now and I don't plan on stopping just because I have Bray in my corner.

I push myself between the two men, facing Bray. He looks at my hands on his chest and a confused look crosses his features, then he brings his eyes to meet mine. "Bray, I need you to let go of the douche, please."

He lets go but does not take his eyes off the guy. He hooks his right arm around my waist and turns to lead me away.

"Wait a sec, I just have to do one thing," I say sweetly to him. He lets go of me. I turn and walk up to the douche and without saying a word, I bring my knee up to meet his balls. He drops to the ground, screaming out curses.

"Okay, now I'm ready to go," I tell Bray and walk past him to Holly, who is still standing on the other side of the table with wide eyes. I grab her hand, pick up both of our purses and walk out of the entrance. I expect Bray to be right behind us, except when I get outside, he's not there.

"What on earth was that, Rye?" Holly asks. "Your date was a douche."

"No, not that part. I got that loud and clear. What on earth have you gone and done to Bray?"

"What do you mean? I haven't done anything." I shrug.

"Rye, that guy really *likes* you, like, *like likes* you." She uses air quotes around all the likes.

"I know." I smile. Because he really does like me. I'm a little fonder of him than I'm willing to admit right now too.

"Rye, he thinks you're his girlfriend. You can't play around with this one. He's practically Alyssa's family now." I know where she is coming from. It's my own fault my twin sister thinks I'm so incapable of having a normal relationship. But I am going to give this a good, hot shot.

Just in secret, mostly.

"I'm not playing around, Holl. We agreed to give the whole exclusive dating thing a go. Bray has this thing about being a boyfriend for the first time ever and he's taking it a bit far, that's all. But we are keeping this under wraps. You can't tell anyone yet. I'm not ready for that."

She nods her head. I know I can trust her—she is the one person other than my mum and dad who I trust with anything. "Sure, I won't tell anyone." Then a huge grin spreads across her face.

"What the hell are you so happy about?" I ask.

"Oh, you know, just that you finally have a steady boyfriend. I honestly never thought I'd see the day. Bray, you are dating Bray, Rye. Have you seen the guy?" Holly waggles her eyebrows up and down.

I laugh. "Yes, I have seen him. All of him. And let me

tell you, if that's the package my future husband comes with, I'm okay with that," I tell her.

"Wait, your future husband? Oh God, please tell me you are not pregnant, Reilly Lili!" Oh great, the teacher voice has made an appearance.

It's also at this precise moment that Bray decides to catch up to us. Can my luck get any crappier?

"I'm certain my boys are good swimmers, babe. I mean, how can they not be." He motions his hands up and down his body, my eyes following their movement. "They aren't good enough to swim through rubber though."

He addresses Holly, "She's one hundred percent not knocked up, Holly."

"Wait, what makes you think you're the only guy who's patted my kitty in the last few weeks?" I ask him. He totally is, but he doesn't know that.

Bray's jaw tightens and clenches, his eyes narrow. Oh, he's mad. I have to work really hard to maintain my poker face and not laugh at his reaction. Then as quickly as he got mad, his cocky ass grin emerges.

"I know you haven't been with anyone else. Any other fucker would pale in comparison to me. You and I both know that, babe." He adds a wink on the end for good measure.

I shrug my shoulders. "*Meh*, I've had better." I fake out boredom.

"Challenge accepted," he says then turns to Holly. "Holly, do you need a ride home?"

"No, thank God. I could not think of anything worse than being stuck in a car with you two lovebirds. I'll see you tomorrow, Rye." Holly hugs me. "Bye, Bray, good luck," she says as she walks over to her car.

Bray grabs my hand, leading me to his car. "You and I are in for one hell of a night, babe. You questioned my manhood—junior was very offended. I'm going to spend all night erasing the memory of any other fucker."

Right, I offended his cock, I'm sure. "*Huh*, you might want to stop off for some energy drinks then, hunny."

As he's about to retort, his phone starts blaring out "Hey Brother" by Avicii. "Sorry, it's Zac. I have to take this," he says, as he answers the call at the same time as he opens my door.

"Yeah?" That's how he answers the call, and that's all I hear of it. He hangs up before he makes his way around the car.

"We have to make a quick stop at the club. Zac's not going in tonight, so I have to do a few things. Do you want me to drop you at my place, or do you want to come with?" he asks. It doesn't escape my attention that dropping me home to my own house was not an option.

"*Ahh*, I'll come to the club. I've got some things to do there anyway."

By the time we make it to the club, I have a whole list of text messages with demands from Zac. Apparently, he's not planning on coming in for a few days, and I need to make sure Bray doesn't burn the place down.

"Does Zac often take days off?" I ask Bray.

"I've never known him to take a day off before. Why?" "Lyssa must be in a worse way than she was letting on

if Zac's staying home with her. I should call her."

"I stayed at Zac's last night. Alyssa hasn't come out of their bedroom yet. I think maybe just give them some time. Zac's not about to let anyone near her right now anyway."

"It's funny you think he would be able to stop me from seeing her." I laugh.

"SHH, I do not want to be caught in here, Bray," I whisper.

We spent the last few hours at the club, each working on our own things. We ended up back in Bray's room at Zac's place. He said something about needing to stay here so he could be around for when Zac needed him. Down came some more of those damn bricks. He is probably one of the most family-oriented men I've met. There is nothing he wouldn't do for his siblings. All three of the Williamson siblings are like that though; they are a very tight-knit crew. Don't get me wrong, I'd do anything for Holly too—she is my ride or die. I'm just learning that there is so much more to Bray than his cocky attitude and good looks, so much more. I'm not too sure my heart can keep up. The more time I spend with him, the more I'm liking the whole boyfriend label.

"Babe, no one is going to hear us, trust me. And if they do, you really think they're going to barge in here?" he asks as he pulls the zip on the side of my dress down.

"Have you met your brother, Bray? Of course, he would barge in here."

"Yeah, he probably would. So, you're going to have to be quiet. Think you can hold in those screams, baby?"

I'm not so sure I can. My body is already on fire, and all he is doing is stripping my dress off. Bray slowly pulls my dress up my body.

"Lift," he commands. I lift my arms above my head, and the dress follows.

Bray drops the dress to the floor and steps back. His eyes travel up and down my body, slowly, so very slowly. My skin erupts in goosebumps; he's not even touching me and yet my body is reacting to him, for him.

"Damn, babe. You had nothing at all on under that dress? All night? And I'm just learning of this now? Next time, I'm going to have to inspect what's underneath your clothing, before we leave the house." He shakes his head.

"I had a dress on Bray, I wasn't naked all night."

"Babe, I don't care that you weren't wearing underwear—you can wear whatever you like. I pity any fucker who thinks they can benefit from your choice of clothing though. I will not hesitate to make sure everyone knows that you're mine, that I'm the one who gets to take you home to bed. That I'm the one who gets to do unspeakable things with this body of yours."

He slowly steps closer to me, trailing his fingertips up and down the inside of my arm, ever so lightly. He's still fully dressed and I'm completely naked. There is something very erotic in that. But that's not what I want right now; what I want is his body. I place my hands underneath his shirt, close my eyes and immerse myself in the feel of his skin—warm and hard. I run my hands over the grooves of his abs, silently counting each one as my hands make their way up to his chest.

"This shirt needs to disappear now," I tell him as I drag my hands back down to his waist.

"Yes, ma'am," he says as he steps back and pulls his shirt over the back of his head. Why that move is so damn sexy, I have no idea. But it is, his biceps bulging with the movements. *Mmm,* I want to lick him all over. The thought *I licked it so it's mine* comes to mind and I laugh a little.

"Not that I don't love hearing your laugh, babe, because I do. But that's not the reaction I was hoping for when I start stripping in front of you."

"Oh, what reaction would you prefer?"

"A *oh my God, Bray, your body is so defined. I can't wait to jump on it and defile you.* Or *wow, Bray, you are the sexiest man I've ever seen.* Something along those lines would suffice."

"Honestly, my first thought was that I wanted to lick you all over, and then I thought—*I licked it so it's mine.* Holly and I used to fight over the last cookie or lollies or whatever, and whoever licked it first got to keep it. So, I want to lick you first, so I get to keep you." I slam my lips shut; I cannot believe I just told him I wanted to keep him.

Bray grabs me by the back of my neck and brings his lips so close to mine and says, "Well, *I've already licked you, babe, so you're mine.* And I plan on licking you a lot fucking more."

I don't get time to respond before his lips are on mine. His tongue pushes its way into my mouth and I greedily take it. I want it all, all of what he has to give.

I need more. I climb his body, literally jump up and wrap my legs around his waist. He doesn't miss a beat, placing his hands on my ass and holding me to him— the rough feel of the denim on my core sending shivers all through me. I attack his mouth and pull his head as close as I can get. No matter how hard I pull or push myself into him, I just can't get close enough.

"*Argh*," I groan. I want more. I don't know what I want

or need at this point. I just know I want more of him.

"Damn, babe, if you keep grinding on me like that, I'm

going to come in my pants like a fucking teenager."

"I don't care. I need more, Bray," I confess.

The next thing I know I'm flying through the air and landing on the mattress. Bray smirks as he stands at the end of the bed, staring down at me. He unclasps his belt buckle.

"How much more, Reilly? Tell me exactly what you want." He unbuttons his jeans, pulling the zip down. I'm so distracted by what he's doing, and by thinking about what's under those jeans, that I forgot what the question was.

"Tell me, Reilly. What. Do. You. Want?" he demands.

I lick my lips, hungry for a taste of him. "I want you to fulfill every fantasy I've ever had, Bray. I want everything."

Bray tilts his head at me and thinks quietly for a bit before finally speaking. "Do you trust me?" he asks.

"With my body, yes. With my heart, no," I answer honestly.

He nods and smirks. "We'll work on your heart another time, because I will win that. I win everything."

Bray removes the belt from the loop of his jeans and holds it in his right hand, dangling down his side. He is the picture of perfection right now. Shirtless, all those tanned, toned muscles on display. Tattoos running up and down his arms and across his chest. There's script across one side of his chest. I'm not close enough to work out what it says, but I plan to read that writing with my tongue as soon as possible. His denim jeans are undone and hanging loose, black briefs underneath with the tip of his cock peeking out the top—shiny metal sparkling at me and begging me to touch it. His voice breaks through my thoughts.

"Will you do everything I say, Reilly?" His question throws me; it's not what I was expecting. I must show my confusion and rebuttal to that thought because he quickly adds, "In the bedroom, right here, right now, will you do everything I tell you?"

Immediately, I reply, "Yes," while nodding my head —maybe a little too eagerly.

Bray's smirk comes out, then his features harden. Something flickers in his eyes. "Good, get on the floor. On your knees, now!"

# CHAPTER TWELVE

BRAY

"GET ON THE FLOOR. On your knees, now!" I demand. I watch as her body visibly shakes from the command. Then like the good little girl she is she gets up, crawls to the end of the bed and climbs down—sitting on the floor right in front of me on her knees.

I wish I had a fucking camera, because this right here is a Kodak moment if I ever saw one. Goddamn beauty like you've never seen before. Her pale skin is flushed and covered in goosebumps. Her full breasts heaving up and down with her panting. Her red hair a tumbled mess down her back. Her green eyes staring up at me, with a mixture of excitement and need.

"Hands behind your back," I command.

She obeys immediately. I don't think she knows just how much she wants to submit to me. I'm not really one for games in the bedroom. I've dabbled with toys and tie downs, etc., but usually it's just a night to get lost in a beautiful woman and get off. With Reilly, it's different though. I want to consume her. I want to be her whole world. I want to make her out of her mind with need for me.

Walking behind her, I pick up both of her wrists. Leaning down, I whisper into her ear, "Good girl." I wrap my belt around her wrists, giving it a tug to ensure they're secure. She won't be getting out of that anytime soon.

I run my hands up her arms and down over the front of her shoulders, until they finally land on her breasts. Filling my hands with the glorious softness, I give her nipples a pinch. Her back arches as she pushes her breasts into my palms. Little moans escape her mouth.

"You need to be quiet, Reilly. You wouldn't want anyone walking in and finding you in this position, would you now?"

She doesn't speak but shakes her head no. Pushing her hair to one side, I lean into her neck and inhale. I can't get enough of her; she smells like a fucking delicious concoction of fruity flavours. I bite down on her neck, then lick over the bite mark to soothe the spot.

She's so fucking responsive, the way she bends her neck further allowing me more access to her delicate skin. I move my left hand down over the smooth skin of her stomach. I don't stop until I reach my target. Using my middle finger, I glide it through the lips of her pussy. She is wet—beyond wet—she's fucking drenched.

"*Ahh*, oh God," she cries out as I tease light strokes over

her and around her clit. Every few strokes, I allow my finger to tease her entrance. As she attempts to move her pelvis out and into my hand, I pull back.

"You're so wet, baby. I fucking love how your body responds to my touch." I continue to pet her pussy for a few more minutes while simultaneously biting down on her neck and tweaking her nipple. I keep my touch light and teasing. I know she's slowly building up to an orgasm. I can feel her body begin to tighten and quake.

"Do you want to come, Reilly?" I ask.

"Oh God, yes, Bray. Don't you dare stop."

"Wasn't planning on it, babe. How bad do you want to come right now?"

"I want it more than you can imagine," she moans out.

I chuckle, I don't need to imagine. I'm getting the show from the front seat. "Beg," I tell her.

"What?" she turns her head looking at me, confused.

"I said beg. You want to come? Beg me to make you come." My tone leaves no room for argument.

"I'm not begging you," she declares. I move my

finger off her pussy and instead stroke it up the inside of her thigh.

"If you want to come, beg," I remind her.

She bucks her pelvis out, trying to realign my finger with her centre. It's not going to work. I want to hear her beg me; I want her to need me, then I want to deliver and prove to her that I'm going to be the one giving her everything she needs from now on.

"Oh. God. Please," she spits out.

I chuckle. I knew she wouldn't be able to hold out on me for long. "Please what, baby? What do you need?" I stop my movements with my finger just millimetres to her clit.

"*Ahh*, God, Bray. Make me come now, damn it!" she yells.

So much for being quiet. "Good girl," I whisper into her ear before clamping down on that sweet spot on her neck just behind her ear. I pull and pinch at her nipple as I slam two fingers into her wet, warm pussy.

"*Mmm*, I fucking love the feel of your pussy. I could leave my fingers buried in here twenty-four seven." Using my thumb, I circle her clit, applying just the right amount of pressure I've come to know she responds to.

"I want you to drench my hand in your juices, Reilly. Come, now." Whether it's a coincidence or not, I don't know, but her body obeys. She screams out my name as her body convulses, her pussy strangles my fingers and she pushes her clit down harder into my thumb. It's a sight of beauty, watching her fall apart.

"Fucking perfect," I tell her after her body has recovered. I remove my fingers and bring them to her lips. "Clean them."

I expect her to recoil or hesitate—she does neither. She sucks the digits between her lips, swirling her tongue around them. Fuck me, she's sucking on my fingers like they're my cock. "See how fucking good you taste? I can't wait to lick your pussy clean before I get it all wet and dirty all over again."

Standing up, she shutters as I make sure she has her balance before I walk around to the front of her. She looks up at me, satisfaction written all over her face.

"You good?" I ask, needing to make sure she's good to continue this play of ours.

"*Uh-huh,*" she answers with a smile and a nod. "Want to keep going?"

"Absolutely," she agrees.

The moment I get her agreement, I slip my shoes off and pull my jeans and briefs off in one swoop. Junior comes bouncing up, standing straight and pointing in the direction of the woman who has captured his sole attention.

Stroking my cock a few times, I step closer to her. "Fuck," I murmur as I watch her lick her full, plump lips. I want those lips wrapped around my cock. "I want to shove my cock down your throat. I want to feel the back of your throat as you swallow me."

She nods at me, giving me the go ahead that she's

on board with the idea. I'm going to need more than a gesture though; I want to hear the fucking words.

"Tell me, Reilly, do you want my cock in your mouth?" I ask her.

She nods her head up and down.

"I'm gonna need you to use your words, Reilly. Tell me, how bad do you want me to put my cock down your throat?"

"Damn it, Bray. I want your cock in my mouth, now. Please." She adds the please onto the end as a second thought.

I smile. "Thought you'd never ask," I tell her as I place my cock at the seam of her lips. Reilly puts her tongue out, licking the tip and swirling around the piercing. Just the slightest touch of her tongue is sending jolts of pleasure through me. I have to force myself not to slam my cock right down her throat.

Inching my cock into her mouth slowly, inch by fucking inch, I realize this is what heaven is. Reilly's warm, wet, welcoming mouth. My attempts to ease in go out the window when she sucks and slides her own mouth all the way down my shaft.

"Fuck Reilly, shit!" I groan as she swallows with my cock in her throat. What the fuck is that sorcery? I slide back out and slam in again, holding her head to keep her steady while gradually picking up the pace. Fuck, if I keep this up, I'm going to come down her throat, which I don't want to do. Well, not this time anyway.

I slow my movements down and pull out of her

mouth. Her lips are swollen and inviting, begging for more of my cock. "Fuck, babe, that mouth of yours is a dangerous weapon," I tell her, picking her up and placing her over the edge of the bed, face down.

She turns her head to look back over her shoulder and smiles at me. "You're welcome."

Stepping between her legs, I nudge them open further with my feet. I kneel down behind her, bringing her pussy in front of my face. I know I should drag this out a bit, but I'm fucking starving for a taste of her. Slowly, my tongue drags from the front of her slit right up to the back.

"*Mmm*, you are the most delicious thing I've ever eaten."

Her body is squirming; I insert a finger just at the entrance of her pussy while pressing my thumb over the bud of her ass. Swirling my tongue around her clit, I keep my fingers still, just applying pressure. Reilly pushes back into my hand, increasing the pressure placed on her two holes, as I continue my torture on her clit.

Her juices run down my hand—she's fucking drenched. "Please, Bray, I need more. Give me more, please." She's begging on her own free will now. I fucking love hearing her beg for me.

Standing up, I pick up my jeans, pull out my wallet and retrieve a condom. "Don't worry, babe. I'm going to give you everything you'll ever need," I tell her while I sheath my cock.

Lining my cock up to her entrance, I wait before pushing in. "Is this friendly vagina of yours going to play nice with junior, Reilly?" I ask with a laugh, not waiting for her answer before I slam into home. I still as my cock bottoms out inside her.

"Fuck me," I grunt. "You're so fucking tight, babe. It's like your pussy is trying to strangle the life out of junior."

I make my movement, sliding out slower and allowing her inner walls time to adjust to the intrusion. Slamming back into her, I grab hold of her hips.

"Hold tight, babe, this is going to be quick and rough," I warn, just before I pick up my pace and slam as hard and fast as I can into her from behind. Her moans are music to my ears, encouraging me to go harder and faster.

"Fuck, I'm going to come. I need you with me, babe," I tell her. Reaching a hand underneath her, I find her clit and press down hard—stroking, pinching and circling.

"Oh God, Bray. I'm..." She doesn't finish her sentence, her body seizing up and going stiff, tremors shaking through her. Her pussy gets even tighter, if that's possible, pulsing and milking my cock as I come right along with her.

I pump a few more times. "Fuck, Reilly."

I'm lost for any other words. I almost fall onto her before I catch myself and roll onto the bed next to her.

Turning to face me, she says, "That was, wow. Just, wow."

"Yeah, it was," I reply while untying the belt from her hands, rubbing both of her wrists, and inspecting for any deep markings. The belt cut into her skin a fair bit, but nothing a bit of arnica cream and some bracelets won't cover.

Picking her up, I lay her under the blankets and climb in next to her before wrapping her up in my arms. Kissing her forehead, I confess, "I really fucking like being your boyfriend, Reilly. I think I've got this gig mastered already."

"I like you being my hidden boyfriend, Bray. What makes you think you've mastered the art of boyfriend in—I don't know, what's it been—five hours?"

I ignore her little *hidden* part, hidden my ass. There is not a soul around who I don't want to scream out at and tell them of my newfound title. "Well, I've got you in my bed completely satisfied from a really fucking good fuck. Now I'm going to spend the night spooning you and holding you as tight as I can, and not just so you can't sneak out on me either. No, I'm going to hold onto you because I actually want to keep hold of you."

"*Mmm*, I wasn't planning on sneaking out," she says around a yawn.

"Go to sleep, babe. I'll still be here holding you when you wake up." I kiss her forehead and settle in next to her, inhaling her sweet, fruity scent.

I have one of the best fucking sleeps I've ever had.

I'm in the gym hitting the weights at five in the morning when Zac walks in and turns the music down. I usually have it blaring while I work out. Zac had the room soundproofed when he got tired of hearing me working out at odd hours. Some nights, when I was younger, I'd spend all night working out just to expel the built-up energy that hit me every now and then.

"Did your house burn down?" he asks. "Nope," I reply and continue my reps.

"Then what the fuck are you doing here at this fucking hour?" He tries to portray that it's shitty I'm here. He's not mad though—I know he'd never say no to having me here.

"I wanted to use your gym, so I stayed here last night," I lie.

"Fuck off, you have a better fucking gym in your own house."

"Yeah, but I was tired after doing your job at your

club last night and didn't feel like driving home." I put the bar down.

Zac doesn't say anything, just stares at me, with those creepy know-it-all eyes of his.

"Fine, I stayed because I was worried about you and Alyssa, okay? Are you happy now, fucker? How is she?" My confession turns his creepy look into one of appreciation.

"She's scared. I had her take two weeks leave from work. We're staying in until after the holidays. I think the safest place for her right now is here."

"Good idea. Anything I can do?" I ask.

"Yeah, find me that fucking bitch. Other than that, try not to burn my club down."

"I'll do my best to keep the club as the pristine and well-oiled machine you have it." I salute his back as he retreats to the door. Just before he opens the door, he turns back to me.

"Oh, and Bray?"

"Yeah?"

"Next time you bring Reilly home, you might want to consider that your bedroom walls are not sound-proof, like these ones."

"Oh, I know." I smirk.

Zac shakes his head. "I won't protect you from Alyssa if you hurt her friend, Braydon."

Oh shit, he brought out the full name shit. I'm actually a little scared of how far he'd go to help her castrate me if she asked. He'd probably do it himself, fucker. "I don't plan on hurting her. I just plan on keeping her," I tell him.

"Sure, that's not the same thing. Poor girl, if she's getting stuck with your crazy fucking ass."

"What can I say? The girls all want to be with me and the boys all want to be me." I shrug as I wipe the sweat from my face with the towel.

# CHAPTER THIRTEEN

REILLY

'VE BEEN SNEAKING AROUND with Bray as much as I possibly can in the last three weeks. The fact that he's been filling in for Zac around the club doesn't hurt—we've found all sorts of closets and offices to get to know each other better.

One time, he even picked me up, threw me over his shoulder and dragged me down to the basement. Let's just say, the three rounds I spent in the cage with Bray, we both came out winners. That man has stamina like I've never seen before. I honestly don't know how he does it. I know he spends all morning working out in Zac's gym. Then he comes into the club and works and still finds time to fuck me senseless every day.

I've managed to avoid being caught sneaking in and

out of Zac's apartment most nights and mornings as well. I thought for sure Zac was more observant and would have caught me by now, but I guess he's so hyper-focused on Alyssa he doesn't know what's going on around him.

The couple of days over Christmas I didn't stay with Bray, I had at least a dozen messages and calls from him, not to mention the late-night video calls. He even managed to get me off over the phone—okay, it was my hands and vibrator doing all the work—but it was his voice and the dirty things he would say that pushed me over the edge every sweet time.

It's New Year's Eve, the club's busiest night I've seen yet. I'm hyper-alert and anxiety riddles my body. Bray's fighting tonight; this is the first fight I have to watch him in since he's been my boyfriend. I'm torn on how I feel about him fighting. On one hand, it's hot as hell, and on the other, I really don't want to see him get hurt.

His cocky ass has assured me that he's winning this fight. It's not his abilities that I question. On some of those nights I've spent in my own bed, without him, I may have spent way more time than necessary watching YouTube videos of his fights. There's also the illegal, underground cage thing that worries me. How he's managed to stay out of jail this long, I have no idea.

I haven't expressed my fears to him, that one day he will be taken away. I've been trying to push those thoughts down and focus on the present. Like right now, I'm sitting in my office staring at a bloody bouquet of doughnuts.

Who the hell sends someone a bouquet of doughnuts? Bray Williamson, that's who. James, the one and only guy in this club who doesn't run the other way when he sees me. James, the bartender well on his way to earning best friend rights. That James, who is also about to get his ass kicked out of my office, is currently sitting on my desk laughing his ass off as he bites into a huge doughnut covered in pink icing and sprinkles.

He's also holding the card that came with the doughnuts out in front of him, as he mocks me, reading it aloud around mouthfuls of food.

"I hope these taste just a sweet as you do. You can eat your sweets now. I'll be devouring mine tonight," he laughs.

"Shut up, asshole, or I won't share any more with you," I warn.

He looks at the box then back up to me. "You can't possibly eat all of these on your own. You need my help, darl."

He's right. I don't know what Bray was thinking. There is no way one person can eat this many doughnuts. They aren't just your typical cinnamon doughnuts—no, these are extravagant. They're huge and in the shape of hearts and circles; some filled with jam, and others covered in icing of all colours and sprinkles. My mouth salivates just looking at the sweet sugary goodness.

"So, who's the guy who's been licking your kitty lately, *huh?*" James questions. "I can't wait till Bray finds out someone beat him to the cookie jar," he laughs.

I'm not quick enough to hide my smirk at his comment. Bray and I, surprisingly, have done a spectacular job of keeping our little relationship secret. The only people who know are my mum and Holly.

"Shut the front door, Reilly Reynolds!" James screeches.

"What?" My innocent *try to play it cool* attitude does not work on him.

"Don't what me! You're fucking Bray! As in, *the* Bray Williamson. Don't even try to lie to me, girlfriend." It's hard not to laugh as he points his half-eaten doughnut at me.

"I don't know what you're talking about."

*Deny, deny, deny.* I keep repeating the mantra in my head. I'm not sure if I'm ready to leave the little bubble Bray and I have created for ourselves just yet. I like that we get to keep us, just us. No one else sticking their two cents into what's happening in our relationship.

Then again, maybe, just maybe, if my friends knew that Bray was mine, they'd stop making remarks about how much they want a turn at the pierced cucumber. When I say friends, I'm talking about Sarah—she's the only one who mentions it really. Alyssa is all about everything that is Zac. As she should be; that man treats her like a damn queen.

He even gave me uncontrolled access to that little

magical black card of his at Christmas. He wanted to get Lyssa a new wardrobe because hers was destroyed by that psycho Caitlyn who has been stalking and tormenting her. I would really love to get my hands on that girl. I know Dean's had teams out searching high and low, but the bitch is a damn cockroach, hiding in nooks and crannies and unable to be found.

Bray has been stressed, spending way more time in the gym every morning than what I think is normal. He says it's because he's preparing for his fight. I've snuck down to the basement here to watch him train a few times. A sweaty, practically naked Bray is a fucking welcoming sight. I've heard his coach tell him he's overdoing it but Bray shrugs him off and says it's temporary.

He doesn't show it, but Bray worries a lot about his family. That's the reason we've been sneaking around Zac's apartment and not just hanging out at Bray's house. Bray wants to be close, in case he's needed. He doesn't trust that Caitlyn won't try something, even while Alyssa is staying in the penthouse with Zac. Neither of them has left the building for a few weeks.

They are both meant to be going back to work tonight, so I'm expecting to see Zac any minute now. Which means I need to get on with my night and get James and these doughnuts away from me.

"Earth to Reilly!" James waves a new doughnut he's holding—this one coated in chocolate icing and white sprinkles.

"What?"

"You were totally zoned out there. Thinking about lover boy Bray?"

"I'm not sleeping with Bray." I try my darndest to continue denying.

"Yes, you are. I don't know why you're not screaming that shit from the rooftops. If I had that boy, I'd be bragging left, right and centre to everyone and anything that would listen. I mean, look at him. He's what wet dreams are made of. Please, for the love of everything that's holy, tell me he is as good in bed as what I've imagined he would be?"

Okay, I know that Bray is one hundred percent about the vagina, but I can't seem to help the green-eyed monster appearing at James's comment. He's been imagining my boyfriend having sex.

"Stop, you need to stop thinking about my boyfriend that way if we are going to remain friends. Or at the very least, never mention those thoughts to me again," I tell him.

The smile that crosses his face is not the scared and intimidated look I was going for. I really need Holly to teach me her teacher voice tactics.

"I knew it!" James jumps up and down like an over-excited kid on Christmas morning. Then I realise the mistake I made, oh crap.

"Wait, you said boyfriend. This is more than I was thinking. I thought for sure you two have been bumping uglies, but I never imagined you'd actually do the impossible and lock down Braydon Williamson. Bloody hell, your vagina must be lined in gold or some shit."

"Are you done?" I ask, waiting for him to calm the fuck down.

"Oh, hunny, I have so much more."

"Well, it will have to wait. I have work to do, so do you."

"At least tell me one thing; inches, what are we talking here?" He holds his hands out in front of him, slowly moving them apart further like he's measuring something.

"You want to know how big Bray's dick is? Go ask him yourself, perv."

"Oh, I have, many, many times. The bastard never gives me a straight answer."

I get up and hold the door open for him, waiting for him to get the hint he needs to leave now. It doesn't take too long. He stands, picking up two more doughnuts before walking out the door.

"This conversation is so not over, girl," he says as I shut the door behind him.

AFTER AN HOUR SITTING in my office, half dreaming and fantasising about Bray and what I want to do to his body tonight, and half focusing on what I need to do for tonight, I get up and head down to the floor. I have one of the hottest bands in—Dawn. They've topped the Australia top thirty charts for three weeks in a row. I knew they would be big. I saw them on YouTube a few months back and booked them in for the New Year's Eve slot.

They released their single four weeks ago, and it blew up big time. I had to get Dean to arrange extra security, because the expected crowd this band is supposed to bring in is beyond what we can actually cater for here. I held off on releasing the tickets for tonight until just two weeks ago. I'm glad I did, because with Dawn's new status at the top of the charts, I priced the tickets higher and they sold out within an hour of being released.

As I'm heading down to the floor, Zac and Dean both rush past me. They don't stop to talk; they are in a zone. Zac looks furious. I wonder who peed in his Wheaties this time. Then it hits me, Alyssa, something is wrong with Alyssa.

I run to catch up with them. The elevator doors shut before I'm even close. Shit. Pulling out my phone, I try to call Alyssa, but the call rings out. Next, I try Sarah. She picks up on the first ring.

"Reilly, oh God, something's wrong. Alyssa's gone," she cries into the phone. My blood runs cold, my fingers tremble and I struggle not to drop the phone.

"What do you mean gone?"

"We were meant to meet for lunch; she didn't show so I called Zac, thinking he was monopolising her time again. Except she wasn't with him. I was going to go into the ER and ask for her, but Zac started tracking her and said she wasn't there and that he was going to find her."

That's a lot to process. "What do you mean he was tracking her? How's he tracking her?" I'm making my way back to my office to grab my things.

"I don't know; he said something about her ring. Oh God, Reilly, what if Caitlyn actually got to her? I feel so helpless right now."

"Zac will find her. If anyone can find her, it's him." I'm not sure if I'm trying to convince myself or her of this. One thing I do know is that Zac will burn the city down in order to find Alyssa. There is nothing he won't do for her.

"Sarah, I gotta hang up. I need to find someone who

can do a semi-decent job of setting up for tonight so I can leave. Find Holly. I'll pick you both up from your place. We are going to find her."

"Okay."

"I'll see you soon," I say before hanging up.

I dial Bray's number. He takes a little longer to answer than Sarah did.

"Babe, is it me or junior who you're missing so soon?" He's overly chirpy for someone who should be going through his pre-fight routine. Which, according to him, is an all-day event, consisting of a deep tissue massage, rub downs and yoga, followed by spending time locked away alone in a room with headphones on and clearing his mind for an hour or two. The whole rub down part did not fly too well with me.

He doesn't sound like he's doing any of that right now though; he sounds like he's in a car.

"Bray, where are you?"

He takes a minute to reply, which tells me he's trying to come up with something. "*Ahh*, I just had to run an errand, babe. I'll be back at the club before you know it."

Run an errand my ass. "What the hell is going on with Alyssa, Bray? Where the fuck is she?" I demand.

He has to know something; he wouldn't have left the club for anything other than an emergency situation. The fact that he doesn't want to tell me just pisses me off more.

"Whoa, babe, calm down. It's going to be okay. I'm

following Zac and Dean now. Zac has a tracker on her; he knows exactly where she is. Dean has some guys who will reach her quicker than we can, and they're already on their way to her. As soon as I know anything else, I'll let you know. I promise."

"Bray, where is she? Where are you heading to?" I want to know exactly where I need to get to. I'm walking out of the club and just about to get in the car.

"Babe, I need you to calm down. You're not driving anywhere while you're in this state."

I laugh. *Does the idiot think he can actually stop me?*

"Either you tell me or I'll find out another way," I say as I start my car.

"Fuck, shit. Reilly, please, you can't drive while you're panicked and freaked out. Turn the car off."

It's pretty clear he's not going to tell me where they're headed to, so I hang up on him.

I dial Sarah back.

"Have they found her?" she asks.

"They know where she is and are heading for her. Bray says Dean has some guys who are close and are on their way to her now."

"Fuck, Reilly, that bitch is crazy as fuck... who knows what she's capable of doing."

"I know. Did you get a hold of Holly?"

"Yeah, she should be here in about five minutes."
"Good, I'll be there in fifteen. Be out front."

"Okay," she says as I hang up.

Shit, now to figure out how the hell we are going to

find where these assholes are heading to. I'm reversing out when someone knocks on the passenger side window, making me jump a mile out of my seat in the process.

"What the fuck, James?" I scream at him as he opens the door and jumps in.

"I've got strict orders to ensure you arrive in Glenvale in one piece, without a hair out of place. Orders directly from Bray. I value my life way too much to not follow those orders."

"Glenvale, what the fuck. That's two hours away, James."

"I'm aware, so let's go. It's only one now, so we'll be able to make it back before the club starts getting busy tonight."

"I have to stop at Sarah's and pick up her and Holly." I reverse out, my hands shaking a little from a mixture of fear and anger. Fear of something happening to my friend and anger that I can't do shit about it right now.

# CHAPTER FOURTEEN

BRAY

*I*'VE BEEN SITTING in this plastic hospital chair for three hours. It's uncomfortable as fuck, and if it were not for Reilly cuddled in next to me with her legs draped over mine, I would more than likely be pacing the waiting room. It's real fucking hard to stay still, my body itching to move. Every time my legs start to jitter, bouncing up and down, Reilly squeezes my hand and looks up at me with concern in her eyes.

I force myself to calm down. I do not want to stress her out any more than she already is. She came barrelling into the hospital about thirty minutes after I got here. She would have broken all sorts of road rules to get here that quickly. The way James would not make eye contact with me confirmed that she was fucking reckless. He was meant to make sure she didn't do anything stupid.

Zac's been in there for an hour with Alyssa—the bastard could come out and give us all an update so we aren't just sitting out here stressing the fuck out.

Dean's been staring at his phone texting God knows who for the last hour. Holly, Sarah and James are sitting opposite Reilly and me, staring at our open show of PDA. Sarah has been switching between questioning—no, not questioning—interrogating us on this sudden development, and pacing the room while cursing out Zac for not coming back out with information.

Holly's been quiet; she's always the quiet observant one of the bunch, but more so now. I want to make sure she's okay, but I know asking her anything in front of the group is not an option—she will pretend everything's fine.

Leaning over and whispering in Reilly's ear, I tell her, "Babe, I'm going to go get coffee. I'm taking Holly with me."

Reilly looks at me confused, then looks across at her sister and nods her head.

"Okay," she says as she untangles herself from me. "Holly, come with me. We're getting coffee." I stand and shake out the stiffness of my legs. I'm really going to need a good fucking massage to loosen up for tonight's fight, that's if I can make it back in time. I don't plan on leaving this hospital until I know Zac and Alyssa are okay.

Holly stands up and grabs her purse, silently following me out. I can tell something is bothering her and I don't like it. Once we are out of ear shot of the group, I say to her, "Whoever it is, give me a name and I'll sort it out."

"What do you mean?" she asks.

"I know you're worried about Alyssa, but you're not yourself. So, whoever it is who's put you in this mood, tell me."

"You don't even know me, Bray. How do you know I'm not always this quiet?"

"I know you better than you think. You're not yourself.

What's wrong?" She's just as stubborn as her sister, but I'm persistent.

"It's you, actually," she says, which has my head snapping in her direction.

"Me, what the fuck did I do?"

"It's you and Reilly. Bray, she hasn't been in a relationship like what you guys have for over five years. She hasn't let anyone in because she's afraid of getting hurt. What's going to happen when you don't want to be tied down anymore? What's going to happen to her when you break her heart? Or do something stupid and end up in jail or something?"

Well, shit, I was not expecting that. I understand her concerns for Reilly but fuck that. I have no plans of letting go of Reilly. If I could convince her to go to Vegas with me right now, I'd be making her Mrs. Bray Williamson.

"Holly, I promise I have absolutely no plans of letting Reilly go anywhere. I'm all in this with her."

Holly observes me for a moment. "Okay, but if you do break her heart, I will come after you. I may be quiet but fuck with my sister, and I will make your life hell."

I smile at the thought of little Holly coming after me. I have no doubt she would find a way to fuck me up if she wanted to. It's always the quiet ones you need to be wary of.

"You can save the crazy for someone else, sweet-heart. I'm not breaking her heart."

"It's about time," Sarah yells out, jumping out of her chair. I look up to see a very exhausted Zac walking into the room while glaring back at her. He's smart enough to hold back whatever he wants to say.

"She's fine; the bullet grazed her shoulder. You can all go back for a minute to see for yourselves, but then you got to go." He leaves no room for argument. Sarah, Holly and James are the first out the door. Zac tells Dean to go with them. "Make sure they don't jump all over her."

Reilly walks up to Zac, wrapping him in her arms. He freezes, unsure what the fuck to do. He looks to me for help, but he's all alone in this one. I just shrug my shoulders at him. I'm close enough to hear what she says, making me fall for her even more. The way she cares for everyone is endearing.

"Thank you for finding her. I'm really glad your over-bearing ass put a tracker in her ring. I'm not even mad about it. I don't know what any of us would do without her. She's extremely lucky to have you, and if you tell anyone I said that to you, I'll deny it to the grave."

Zac returns her hug and says, "Thank you," as she releases him.

"I'll catch up with you, babe." I give her the indication to go ahead without me. I want to make sure that Zac is okay.

I wait for Reilly to be out the door before I ask, "You doing okay, man?"

Zac runs his hands through his hair. "I've never been so terrified in my life."

"I know, but she's okay, right? And Caitlyn's been taken care of." I don't really know what to say. He's usually the one giving me the pep talks, not the other way around.

"Yeah, thank fuck. There is something else though." "What?"

"Alyssa's pregnant," he says with a huge fucking smile plastered across his face.

Okay, so obviously this is a good thing. Thank fuck, they could use some good. "Congratulations! That's great. Obviously, you're chuffed about this development but how's Lyssa feel?"

"She's okay. When the doctor told us, my stomach dropped. She didn't want kids, Bray. The one thing she told me she didn't want and I went and knocked her up anyway."

I raise my eyebrows at this. I didn't know Lyssa didn't want kids. "What do you mean you knocked her up anyway? Did you intentionally get her pregnant?" I ask, appalled.

I would never think that he would do something like that, but he's fucking insane over this girl so who the fuck knows what he's capable of.

"Fuck no, I would never do that. It was an accident. An accident that we are both thrilled about now," he claims.

Yeah, my perfectly calculated, never makes a mistake brother, accidentally knocked up his fiancée. I'm still doubting that it was not intentional.

"Bray, fuck you. I did not knock her up intentionally. I can't help it. I lose my mind and all sense of responsibilities when she's around."

Yeah, that's the more likely story. She does make him go fucking stupid, but in the best way. She's the best thing to happen to him.

"I don't really care how you got her knocked up," I lie

—I totally would have kicked his fucking ass if he did that to Lyssa. "I'm going to be an uncle, finally. Jeez, it took you long enough, bro. I thought I'd be sixty before you made me an uncle."

"Shut up, idiot. Let's go see her so I can kick all those fuckers out."

I slap him upside his head. "What the fuck was that for?"

"One of those fuckers happens to be my girlfriend—watch how you talk about her."

He laughs. "Your girlfriend? When did that happen?" "A few weeks back. We've just been keeping it on the

DL. You know, sneaking around like teenagers." I wiggle my eyebrows up and down.

"I wish you fucking snuck around as a teenager with the number of times I had to call cabs for girls you'd leave asleep in your bed. Why the fuck would you start sneaking around now?"

"Please, you only saw a fraction of the girls I brought home, most of them were gone before morning even broke. Besides, it's Reilly who wanted to keep us on the DL, not me. I'd be shouting it from the rooftops, that she was mine."

"Yeah, I can see why she wouldn't want it made public that she's with your ass," the fucker laughs; to which, I slap him up the backside of his head again.

We make it to Lyssa's room. Walking in, I can see all three girls hovering over her, Dean attempting to tell them to move back. Not one of them is listening to a word he says. James, however, is the smart one, standing on the opposite side of the bed, not touching Alyssa at all.

I squeeze my way through the three of them, effectively pushing them out of my way. "Stand clear, I'm coming through," I declare.

"What the fuck, Bray!" Sarah screeches, while both Holly and Reilly give me death glares.

"What makes you think you can just barge your way in?" Reilly questions.

"I'm her favourite brother-in-law. Trust me, babe, she wants to see me. Don't you, Lyssa?" I look down at her. She's laughing, but I can see the torment in her eyes from the hellish day she's had.

"Of course, I want to see you," she laughs.

"Told you so!" I say to Reilly, who just shakes her head at me.

I lean down and kiss Alyssa on the forehead and Zac makes a big deal of clearing his throat. Jealous bastard can't stand anyone touching her.

"You doing okay, sweetheart?" I ask her. "I am now," she smiles.

"Good. Now, do you need anything before your grump of a fiancé kicks us all out?"

"No, I'm good. But you should get going. Don't you have an ass to kick tonight?"

"Yeah, I do." I look down at my watch. The fight is still four hours away; I can make it back in time.

I can hear Reilly groan behind me. She doesn't say anything though. I'm sure whatever it is, I'll hear about it the moment we're alone.

Leaning down, I whisper into Lyssa's ear, "Thank you for making me an uncle. This baby is going to be loved like no other, I promise you." Standing back up, I see tears running down her face. Shit, now I've gone and done it.

"Fuck, Bray. I'm gonna kick your ass for making her cry," Zac growls out. I don't get time to rebut his statement before Reilly and Holly both stand between Zac and me. At the same time, they both say, "Touch him and I'll cut your damn balls off, Zac."

The whole room goes silent. Well, all the men in the room go silent. Sarah and Lyssa are desperately trying not to let their laughter escape. I don't know why they're laughing—that shit's straight out of *Children of the Corn* kind of scary. I'm dumbfounded, looking between the two of them. I can't see their faces as they're facing Zac. But I'm sure I don't need to see them. I know the expression they are both wearing, identically.

Zac looks over their heads at me. "Yeah, good luck with that, mate," he laughs.

I'm still a little shocked. I don't think I've ever had a girl stand up for me like that, other than Ella. Not just one, but both of them. "*Ahh, babe,*" I say, pulling Reilly around to look at me. "I appreciate you sticking up for me, but I can handle him all on my own."

She laughs, "Bray, you look like you've seen a ghost." "Well, that shit you two pulled just then is fucking

freaky, okay?" Reilly and Holly look at each other and smile; they both then turn to me and say, "Freaky? Really? Bray the fighter is scared of us two little twins?"

"Okay, stop. Now. That's not fucking funny." I grab Reilly's hand and start pulling her towards the door, as everyone else in the room is laughing. "Reilly we're going." As I get to the door, I dig my keys out of my pocket and throw them to James. "Make sure Holly gets home without a scratch, and Sarah, well, just make sure she makes it home?" I laugh and duck the bottle of water she throws at my head.

Reilly stops, picks up the water bottle, and throws it back at Sarah. "Don't throw shit at him, Sarah," she says before walking out. Everyone in the room looks at me.

Holly laughs and says, "Boy, she has it really bad." At that, I smirk. I like that my girl is feisty and protective.

REILLY HAS BEEN silent pretty much the whole two hours it took to drive back to the club. Before I let her out of the car, I need to find out what's bothering her.

"Okay, what's wrong?" I ask. "Nothing's wrong."

"Something's wrong. Tell me. I can't fix it if you don't tell me, and we both know I'm not going to stop bugging you until you tell me."

"I'm worried, that's all," she says.

"About Lyssa? She's going to be fine." I try to reassure her.

"Not Alyssa, you."

"Why the fuck are you worried about me?" I ask, dumbfounded.

"You're going to fight tonight, you haven't exactly been prepping all day, and you haven't done your pre-fight routine things. What if you're not ready?"

"Babe, this ain't my first rodeo. Trust me, I know what I'm doing."

"I know you can fight, but what if tonight's the one

time that it goes wrong? I just don't want you to get hurt, that's all."

I pull her over the centre console and sit her on my lap so she's straddling me. "I promise I'll be careful. I'll be focused. There is nothing in this world that can take me away from you, okay? I will always fight for us, Reilly. We are worth fighting for."

I gently lay kisses all over her face, and her body relaxes and sinks into me. "I'll fight for us too, Bray. I won't let anyone take you from me," she says before slamming her lips onto mine and claiming more and more of my heart and soul.

# CHAPTER FIFTEEN

REILLY

*J*'M SITTING in the front row of the ring with Dean on one side of me and a hulky beast of a man on the other. I don't know what his name is; he won't talk to me anyway. I'm anxious as hell, waiting for Bray's fight to come on. His is the last one of the night—the main event—as he likes to inform me. He's the fucking star, his words not mine.

I've watched three fights so far. Each one bloody, messy and always ending with someone knocked out on the floor. I send a little prayer up—please, God, don't let that be Bray. I've just found him. I can't lose him now.

The last fight ended about five minutes ago; the

basement is full of people. The crowd is loud, people shouting from all directions. I stay seated, glued to the spot and wait.

Dean leans over, trying to calm me. "You know he's literally the best fighter, right? You have nothing to worry about, Reilly."

"No wonder his ego is so big, if you're all going around talking about him like he's some kind of god," I yell back.

"Isn't he?" Dean says with his eyebrows drawn. "Because he's been telling me he is for at least ten years now. He's said it so often I think he brainwashed us all into believing it."

I laugh. Damn, Dean actually cracked a joke. I've only ever seen serious Dean, never this playful side. I think I like the playful side better. This must be what Ella sees.

I know they think no one knows about their little budding friendship, but I know. Bray knows, but doesn't want to know. The only one who doesn't know is Zac; he's too blinded by everything that is Alyssa to notice. I really hope I'm around to watch that shit show unfold.

I'm brought out of my own head from the lights dimming and the music that starts blaring "T.N.T" by ACDC. This is Bray's entrance song. I remember hearing it the first time I saw him fight here.

He comes prancing out, alone this time. There are

no card girls hanging off him. They do appear a few steps behind him. They're not touching him though, which is good... for them. I don't share very well.

I watch and can't help but smile as Bray dances and shows off his muscles as he makes his way to the cage. He's just about to the door when he stops, turns and runs the few steps towards me. Grabbing me by the back of my neck, he kisses the ever-loving hell out of me. The noise of the crowd and music fades as I get lost in him. Breaking the kiss, he leans down and whispers in my ear, "I fucking love you, Reilly."

My eyes widen, my mouth hanging open. Bray smirks and makes his way back to the cage. *What the hell just happened?* By the time I recover from shock, Bray is prancing around in the cage, his eyes never leaving me for very long. I smile at him and he winks back.

His opponent is in the cage, although not getting anywhere near the fanfare that Bray is receiving.

The bell goes and before I know it, the fight has started; both men knock gloves with each other. Right away, Bray's opponent takes a swing at his head, which Bray dodges and returns an uppercut to the guy's ribs.

I watch as both men go back and forward at each other, and I try not to squeal as Bray takes hits all over his body. The bell for the first round goes and the fighters take their corners. I can see Bray's coach yelling at him and Bray shaking his head no. There is blood dripping down his face that someone else is wiping off with a towel.

When the second round starts, it's much of the same, each fighter giving and taking blows, kicks, etc. The opponent gets an upper hand, slamming Bray into the cage, pinning him there, and landing blow after blow all over his body. I go to get up—to do what, I don't know—but I see red. I want to strangle this asshole who thinks he can hurt Bray.

Dean's quick to pull me back down. "Settle down, Harley Quinn, your man is more than capable of taking care of himself." As the words come out of Dean's mouth, Bray pushes back, gets his opponent pinned to the ground and slams his fist into the side of his head. The ref leans down and blows his whistle before yelling something out.

The crowd goes wild. Bray stands, leaving the other guy laid out flat on the ground. The medics rush in to help him. Bray's arm is held up and he's walked around the cage. He won. Thank God, he's not the one laid out on that floor.

Bray shakes off the ref and climbs out of the cage. He heads straight for me and lifts me up. I wrap my legs around him and just before I let my lips meet his, I tell him, "I fucking love you too, Braydon Williamson."

I don't know how he manages it, but Bray carries me out of the basement and into his dressing room while delivering the most delicious kisses. He turns on the shower and doesn't put me down. Instead, he slams my back into the wall and grinds his hard cock right onto my clit.

"*Argh...* God... that... keep doing that," I beg. I'm not ashamed to beg him for what I need anymore. I know he'll always deliver and he gets off on hearing me beg him. So, win-win in my eyes.

He breaks the kiss and drops my feet to the floor. I groan, "Really? Now you put me down?"

"I need you fucking naked, now, Reilly. Strip," he commands.

Taking a step back, he watches my every movement. My whole body shivers and my core pulses and weeps at his commanding tone. I don't waste time in getting my dress over my head. I unclasp the black lace bra and let it fall to the ground. Next, I slip out of my pumps and slide my matching panties down my legs before straightening back up and waiting for my next command; because I know there will be one.

"Goddamn, you are fucking gorgeous."

Bray drops his briefs to the ground, releasing his rock-hard cock. My mouth waters at the sight. I don't dare move until he tells me what to do, though.

We've been playing this way long enough that we both know the game. I've never been with anyone that I wanted to dominate me before, or boss me around. But, when Bray does it, damn, that shit is hot as hell.

As I'm raking my eyes up and down his body, my

mind is cataloguing the damages he received from the fight. His ribs are bruising on both sides, he has a nasty mark on the outside of his left thigh and his face, well, it's seen better days—that's for sure. I'm about to ask him if maybe he should be seeing a doctor, or medic, when he speaks first and I get distracted by that damn pierced cucumber again.

"Do you want to play, Reilly?" Bray asks while stroking his hand up and down his cock. That should be my hand. I should be touching, stroking, licking that cock.

"Yes," I answer and nod my head, not able to take my eyes off his cock.

"Good girl, get in the shower under the water, hands on the wall." I follow his instructions, step under the warm water and place my hands on the wall. I turn back to look at him and wait for my next command. I can feel the slickness of my pussy dripping down my thighs already.

Bray silently walks up behind me, and out of nowhere a loud smack lands right on my ass. "*Ahh, fuck, God.*" The sting follows the sound; the pleasure follows the sting.

"Did I say you could turn around?" Bray asks as he delivers another delicious slap to the other side of my ass.

"*Ahh,* oh, fuck me. No, you didn't, Bray," I reply between moans.

"That's right, I didn't. Face the wall. Do not move until I tell you to, or I won't let you come."

I smirk at that; we both know that's one thing he can't help, making me come as many times as I possibly can.

Bray reaches around, pinching both of my nipples between his fingers while biting down on my neck. He knows just the spot to bite down on that drives me freaking crazy. My body is on fire, my nerve endings short circuiting, as pleasure rolls through me. My skin is tingling all over and my pussy is pulsing with need while seeking what she needs—Bray's cock filling her up. "Fuck, Bray, don't stop."

"Never going to, babe," he declares. He lets my right breast go as he trails his hand down past my stomach. Just as I think I'm in luck and he's going to go straight for my clit to put me out of this beautiful torture, his hand goes around the back of my thigh. He grabs my leg and pulls on it, effectively spreading my legs further apart.

"I worked up an appetite out there, babe. I'm fucking starving."

"*Uh-huh.*" I don't know what he expects me to say. I don't even know if I'm capable of coherent words right now.

"Are you going to be a good girl for me, Reilly, and stay still while I eat?"

"Yes." I nod my head. I'm not really sure what I've

just agreed to. Is he going to leave me standing here waiting for him?

"Perfect, you're so fucking perfect," he says as his body slides down behind me. He bites on my right butt cheek.

"Oh, fuck." I push my ass out further against his skin. It freaking hurts but the pleasure that rolls through me at the same time is unlike anything else I've ever felt.

"*Mmm*, I'm going to feast on you until you have nothing left to give, until I've drained you dry."

Bray swipes his tongue from the top of my pussy right up to my ass. He holds me still, his hands spreading my cheeks wide. His tongue delves into my pussy, swirling around, while his fingers flex on my skin. He brings his mouth up to my clit and sucks hard, occasionally twirling his tongue around. I'm not doing a great job at standing still, pushing myself harder into his face.

He inserts two fingers into my core, circling around my G-spot and causing me to cry out. "Oh, fucking, Bray, God. *Ahh*." I see stars and struggle to stay upright.

I can feel an orgasm coming on, my body begins to violently shake, and I'm chasing this bitch like my life depends on it. I can feel it; it's so close. "I'm so close."

One of his fingers starts rubbing around my rear bud, circling and sending all sorts of new sensations through me. That finger then pushes its way in, slowly pushing further and further until it's buried all the way inside my ass.

My core and ass are both clenching onto his fingers, his mouth still sucking on my clit. He slowly pumps his fingers in and out of both holes. I feel like my whole body is about to explode. I come screaming his name.

The only thing holding me up right now is Bray's arm around my waist. I come back down to earth as one of his hands is caressing my breast, the other still pumping fingers slowly in and out of my pussy.

"Welcome back," Bray's gravelly voice says into my ear.

"*Mmm*, thank you." I can feel the pleasure building again already as his fingers work their way in and out of my pussy.

"I need my cock buried in this pussy of mine, now," Bray says, removing his fingers and lining himself up with my entrance.

I don't give him time to slowly work his way in and torture me in the process. As soon as I feel his cock lined up, I push myself back and slam down onto him.

"Fuck," we both say at once.

"Goddamn, Reilly. Warn a guy next time. I just about came right then. You feel so fucking good, babe."

I laugh. There's no way he's a one pump dump. He's a fucking machine, can last for hours like he's running off Energizer batteries or something. Once he's sure I've had time to adjust to him being buried deep inside me, he starts to move. Slowly at first, building up his speed and thrusts until he is slamming into me from behind.

The metal of his piercing hits my G-spot, over and over again. I freaking love this piercing; it never fails to hit the spot. I have come multiple times because of this piercing. I can feel how wet I am, wetness gushing out and running down my thighs as Bray continues to slam into me.

His thumb starts circling my ass. I feel him slide it down between our bodies, covering it in my juices before going back to my ass and inserting it. He keeps it still and it's fucking torture. I don't know what his obsession with my ass is lately, but I'm not complaining. It's a strange foreign feeling. With his cock in my pussy, and his thumb in my ass, I feel full, with sensations going haywire in my body.

I need him to move that finger though; I pump my hips back and forward, getting little movement of my ass on that finger. Bray is relentless though; he's slamming his cock into me, but won't move that finger.

When he finally starts moving his finger a few minutes later, it causes me to come again—screaming the place down. Again. Bray pulls out and I feel him spurt all over my back.

"Fuck, fuck, fuck, Reilly," he groans out as he comes, milking himself on my back. "I fucking love fucking you," he continues, straightening me up and spinning me around. He wraps a hand around my throat, pushing me against the wall as his lips connect with mine. Our tongues fight for power, and I struggle to overpower him. He wins though—he always wins. I let him take control of the kiss.

His hand around my throat tightens and closes; I moan into his mouth. As he picks me up, my legs wrapping around his waist, he lines his cock up and enters me in one swift motion. I told you—he's a damn Energizer Bunny.

# CHAPTER SIXTEEN

*Bray*

THE LAST WEEK has been fucking perfect. I've had Reilly at my house, no more sneaking around, no more staying at Zac's place. Alyssa is doing great; somehow Zac convinced her to quit her job and help him out at the club instead. Although from what I've heard from Reilly, Zac's not letting her actually do much at all, which is driving Lyssa insane.

Reilly's come a long way in accepting our relationship as something that is set in stone and here to stick. Her walls are completely down, finally. I thought I'd have to take a damn sledgehammer to those fuckers.

I've tried to talk her into moving in, but she's staying strong on that refusal. I will wear her down eventually. I get she doesn't want to leave her mum and sister, but everyone has to leave the nest eventually. I offered to buy a house on the same street for her mum; she laughed at me and told me I was crazy and to not even think about doing something stupid like that.

Considering their home holds a lot of sacred memories, I would never dream of moving her mum out of there. I do however want to move Reilly out, and straight into my house. I didn't buy this big fucking house to live here alone forever.

I bought it, knowing I wanted to settle down one day, to have ten kids running around. I think I'll wait till after she has my name to bring that up though. For the moment, I'm fucking stoked at the thought of being an uncle.

I've just finished working out in my home gym. Reilly went to work a while ago. I don't like when she leaves, but I'm not a clingy fucker like Zac; I know how to let go for a few hours. Besides, I fell in love with exactly who she is, and an independent workaholic is exactly who she is. Why would I change anything about her or try to get her to change? Besides, you can't improve on perfection, and Reilly is fucking perfection in the finest form.

Walking into my kitchen, I find Ella sitting at the counter with a cup of tea in her hands. I'm surprised to see her; she hasn't been around much lately. I walk up and give her a sweaty hug and kiss on her head.

"Hey, princess, I missed you."

"*Eew*, Bray that's gross. Get off me. You stink," she squeals and pushes me off her.

"Well, princess, if you don't want long drawn-out welcomes, don't take so long to visit. Where have you been, anyway?"

"Busy," she replies.

I grab a bottle of water from the fridge and down it while staring her down. Once I finish the water, I lean against the counter near where she is sitting.

"Elaborate, Ella. What does busy entail?"

"Nothing much. Just hanging with friends, you know, getting ready to start uni, that sort of thing," she shrugs.

"*Uh-huh*, so why have you been avoiding me?" I've only seen her in passing here and there. Normally, she'd spend a couple of nights a week here with me. Even when I stayed at Zac's for those few weeks, I barely saw her around.

"I'm not avoiding you, just giving you space. No one wants their little sister being the third wheel to their new relationship."

Shit, she thinks she has to stay away because of my relationship with Reilly? That's not happening.

"Ella, you'd never be the third wheel, and you're never in the way. You know that, right? You can come here whenever you want. You're my favourite sister so you will always have a place wherever I am." The more I think about it, the more furious I am with myself for not realising she was feeling like she couldn't be around here.

"Bray, I'm your only sister, idiot. And I know I can come here, but honestly, I've just been busy."

"Well, as long as you know that I don't ever want you to stay away because you think you need to." I get the feeling there is more that she isn't telling me. What else is going on with her?

"I know. Thank you."

"Want something to eat? I'm starving and you look like you haven't eaten a cooked meal in forever. Has that idiot brother of ours not been feeding you?"

"Zac's not an idiot, and you know he has a chef cook our meals. God, could you imagine him in a kitchen actually making anything other than coffee?"

I laugh, because it's true. Zac could burn water—he's that useless in the kitchen. "That's true, but if everyone was good at everything, well, then everyone would be me."

"Sure, master of all. Whatever you say." She salutes me.

"Come on, Ella, you and I both know I'm your most talented and favoured brother; the sooner you admit it, the sooner you can put Zac out of his misery and he can stop competing for that spot."

"*Huh*, actually I think Zac has taken the number one spot. After all, he is the one making me an aunty."

"Fuck, do you think Reilly would be on board with the plan of getting knocked up?" I ask her seriously.

"Nope." She annunciates the P sound.

"No, probably not. It is pretty cool that we are getting a niece or nephew soon."

"Yeah."

I dig through the fridge, pulling out sandwich fillings, and end up making chicken and salad rolls for us. As I'm putting it all together, Ella finally spills what's bugging her.

"Bray?"

"Yeah?"

"Why would a guy not want me? I mean, is there something wrong with me that repels men?"

*Let's fucking hope so*, I think to myself. "You own mirrors, right? I know you do. You are fucking beautiful, Ella, inside and out. If some douche is not seeing that, then that's on him not you." It then hits me that she said men, not one particular guy. "Wait, men as in plural, or one man in particular? What are we talking about here?" I ask, needing to clarify just how many men she thinks are repelled by her.

"There's one guy, but he won't even give me a second glance. I thought maybe he felt something, but apparently it's one-sided." She looks fucking heartbroken. I want to go and beat the shit out of the fucker who's making her feel less than worthy.

"Who is it? I need a name, Ella," I demand, handing her a pen and paper.

She shoves the paper back at me. "You will go to your grave waiting on that name, Bray."

She's not going to tell me. "You know I'll find out

anyway. You should just make it easier on both of us and fess up, little sister."

Ella stands up. "Nice chat, Bray, but I've got plans. See you later."

Following her out to the door, I wait for her to open it before I say, "Make sure you tell Dean I said hi."

Ella freezes, the door half open, before she turns around with her mouth hanging open. I got the reaction I was looking for, the confirmation that there is something going on between him and Ella.

"I'm going to fucking kill him." My blood is boiling. I suspected that he was fooling around with Ella for a few weeks now. She's just confirmed it for me.

"No, you're not. You are going to shut your mouth and not say a damn word to anyone, Braydon," Ella shouts at me.

I laugh, "You expect me to do nothing while my eighteen-year-old little sister sneaks around with my brother's best friend, who happens to be fucking twenty-eight?" I yell back.

"We're not sneaking around, Bray. Nothing is happening. Like I said, I'm not worthy enough to be noticed." I see the tears forming in her eyes.

"Wait, Dean's the fucker who has you questioning yourself? What did he do, Ella?" I'm doing my best to hold back my temper I can feel bubbling at the surface under my skin.

"Nothing, that's the thing, Bray. He. Won't. Do.

Anything! No matter how hard I try, he won't touch me. He's too damn loyal to Zac or some shit like that."

I pull her into my arms. "Ella, you're eighteen. You need to experience life before you settle down. I can't believe I'm saying this, but Dean is a fucking idiot if he doesn't see what a catch you are. About to be a dead fucking idiot, but an idiot all the same."

"Bray, you can't touch him. It's humiliating enough. Plus, I love him and if you hurt him, I will hate you forever." She pulls out of my arms. She can't mean that, can she? By the look in her eyes, it hits me she does.

"Fuck, Ella, okay. I won't touch him, but I want you to promise me one thing."

"What?"

"I want you to go to uni, meet some new friends. Experience everything that life has to offer. Don't waste time or energy on any man who isn't worth it. And any man who would choose their friend over you is not worth it."

"I'll try; it's not like I actually have a choice. I can't force someone to love me back."

She walks out the door, slamming it behind her. Fucking Dean, what the fuck is wrong with him?

Getting out of the shower to Zac blowing up my phone is not how I wanted the rest of my day to go. I don't bother answering, choosing to get dressed first. The second I walk into my closet, his ringtone, that stupid fucking song he programmed into my phone, starts blasting through the room again.

"What do you want?" I answer. "Where are you?"

"At home, why?"

"We have an issue at the club, wanted to make sure you weren't here somewhere."

My blood runs cold... Reilly is at the club right now. "What kind of issue and where the fuck is Reilly?"

I walk into my closet and throw on a pair of grey sweats and a white shirt. I slip my feet into a pair of joggers before grabbing my keys and wallet. I'm out the door in less than two minutes.

"Bray, stay the fuck where you are. Reilly is fine. She's in my office."

Like I'm going to stay here. Does he not know who

the fuck he's talking to? "What's going on, Zac? Start fucking talking," I yell.

"I start the car and switch him over to the Blue-tooth." "Jesus, Bray, I told you to stay the fuck where you are.

You do not need to be here. We have it handled."

The fucker still has not divulged what is going on and I'm losing my patience. I'm at least a thirty-minute drive away from the club.

"What have you got handled, Zac?"

"Stephen, the lead singer from Cyrus, the one you put in the hospital a few weeks back, turned up with a bunch of guys looking to start problems. Like I said, the last thing I need is to be fetching your ass out of jail right now, so stay where you are."

"I'm not going to sit here like a fucking pussy, Zac. If he's looking for trouble, I'll fucking deliver it."

"Why the fuck do you always have to be so fucking stubborn, asshole? What do you think Reilly will do when she sees your ass being taken away in cuffs again?"

Well shit, I can't let that happen. Not after how far we have come. How hard it's been for her to let down her guard. But fuck if I'm going to sit here while my girl is in that building with a bunch of assholes.

"I won't do anything that will see me in cuffs, Zac. Scout's promise."

"You were never a fucking Boy Scout, Bray. Look, I

gotta go. Dean and the boys have this sorted out. Do not just barge in here guns blazing!"

I MAKE it to the club in just under twenty minutes, and pull up to the back door. I don't waste any time making my way through the back rooms to the main floor. The scene I'm greeted with has me wanting to choke the life out of someone, whoever the fuck thought they could come into our club and do this.

The club is trashed; it looks like a damn tornado has been through here. Chairs thrown and broken everywhere, tables turned up, all the curtains that line the walls ripped to shreds. Glass litters every inch of surface space. I spot Zac, sitting at the bar, nursing a glass of whisky, and holding an ice pack to the right side of his face.

He's in one piece at least. Looking around, I can't see Reilly anywhere. "Where the fuck is she?" I yell, directing the question at Zac.

He lifts his arm and points behind me. "Over there, in one piece, so calm the fuck down."

Spinning around, I see Reilly at the far end of the bar, broom in hand and sweeping up pieces of broken glass. I stalk my way through the debris of furniture and glass until I reach her. Taking the broom out of her hand, I throw it off to the side before pushing her against the bar and crowding her space. I grab her face in both hands, holding her still as my lips connect with hers.

I pour everything into this kiss, all my pent-up rage, all my fear of something happening to her and my thankfulness that she's unharmed. Reilly gives just as much to this kiss—she's completely open to me now. I succeeded in annihilating her walls, there are no more barriers between her and me, and I fucking love it. I fucking love her.

Pulling back from the kiss, I lean my forehead against hers. "I fucking love you."

"*Mmm*, I love you too," she replies, breathless.

"Are you okay?" I ask as I do a visual inspection of her from head to toe. "I don't know what I'd do if something happened to you, babe. Actually, I do know. I'd burn this town to the ground until I found the fucker I needed to kill."

Her body goes stiff under my touch. Fuck, I should have kept that thought to myself, even if it is the truth. "Babe, I'm sorry. I shouldn't have said that out loud."

"Bray, I don't ever want you to go after anyone

because of me. Do not throw your life away because of me, ever."

"I don't have a life without you anymore, Reilly. I will always fight for us, even if I have to find new ways to fight."

"I know." She leans into me.

I look around—this is going to be one hell of a clean-up bill.

"If you two lovebirds are finished, I need Reilly," Zac says as he approaches.

"What for?" I ask. The bastard ignores me, instead talking directly to Reilly.

"We're all going to Hawaii. Book a jet for tomorrow morning. Alyssa and I are getting married."

Reilly lets go of me and faces Zac. I don't like it. With a slight growl, I pull her back against my chest, wrapping my arms around her middle. Zac smirks at me.

"Wait, does Alyssa know about this? You can't just decide you're getting married tomorrow without discussing it with her first. What if she doesn't want to get married in Hawaii? *Huh*? Have you even thought of that?"

Zac holds up his finger, indicating for her to wait, while pulling his phone out and placing it on speaker.

"Zac, this baby is making me bloody horny as hell. Hurry up and get home already please," Alyssa answers the phone.

Reilly bursts out laughing. Zac just looks pained, more pained than he did icing his bruised face.

"Great, I'm on speakerphone, aren't I? Thanks for the warning, Zac."

"Ignore them, sunshine. I'll be there as soon as I can. I just need to handle a few things at the club, but I wanted to run something past you?"

"Sure, hit me."

"Tomorrow morning we're flying to Hawaii, you, me and unfortunately our family and friends. We're getting married. Any objections?"

Alyssa's squeal stings my ears. All the guys around us, who were going about their business, stop and look over at the commotion coming out of Zac's phone.

"Oh my God! Zac, Oh, my gosh. Yes, yes, yes! Let's do this. I can't bloody wait to be Mrs. Zac Williamson," Alyssa continues to squeal through the phone.

"Sunshine, I can't wait either. I'll be home soon." Zac hangs up the phone, raising an eyebrow at Reilly with a huge smile on his face.

"Okay, no need to be so bloody smug about it. Where abouts in Hawaii? Do I need to book a hotel? And why don't you have a PA to handle this sort of shit? This is not in my job description, you know." Reilly is getting fired up. I can feel the energy coming off her.

"Settle down, just book the jet. Everything else will be handled," he says as he starts typing into his phone. No doubt to delegate tasks off to others.

"Okay, I'll be upstairs. Make sure you come and see me before you leave," Reilly says, leaning up to offer a parting kiss.

"I'm not leaving this building without you, babe. I'll come up in a little bit."

I watch as she walks away, the sway of her hips in that tight skirt taunting me the whole way.

"I need you to organise a reschedule for Friday's fight. One, you're not going to be here. Two, I'm shutting the club down for renovations, obviously."

"Sure, I'll get on that, just as soon as you tell me what the fuck happened in here," I demand.

"They came in, about thirty of them with baseball bats, and went ballistic smashing the place up. Dean called in the cavalry and we cleared them out."

"So, how many bodies need to be disposed of?"
"None."

"None? You're telling me, some motherfuckers came in here and did this." I wave my arms around. "And you didn't kill any of them?" I don't believe it.

"What can I say? We're turning over a new leaf, Bray. I can't risk not being around for Alyssa and this baby. We need to start handling things in more legit ways."

"I agree, things have been changing. What about Club M?" I ask. I honestly don't know what I'd do without fighting. Could I go professional on the up and up? Probably. Do I want to? Absolutely not. I also don't want to give up fighting.

"I'm not sure yet, but we do need to think about changing that up too. It was okay to take the risks when it was just me who would go down. I can't do that to Alyssa, Bray. She's never had a proper, safe family and I intend to give her that."

"I get that, man, I do. I just don't know what to do with myself when I'm not fighting."

"I know, but even you can't fight forever, Bray. Whatever you need to do, you know I'll be there, no matter what."

"Yeah, thanks, bro. Don't worry about me. I'll figure it out. Besides, have you met me? I'm like the fucking king of all trades, excel at everything I do."

"Whatever helps you sleep at night." Zac gets the hint that I'm not fully ready to discuss me not fighting anymore. Thankfully, he drops the topic.

"So, what are we gonna do about this mess?"

"It's being handled. We are going to Hawaii, and I am getting married to a fucking goddess. By the time we come back, this place will have had a facelift."

"Right, I'll see you on the tarmac tomorrow morning then," I say, walking away and leaving him to it.

"Don't be fucking late, Bray. I will leave without you," he yells out at me.

Turning, I smirk. "No, you won't. Lyssa would never let you get married without her favourite brother-in-law there."

I laugh at his cursing while I walk away.

# CHAPTER SEVENTEEN

REILLY

"$\mathcal{I}$ CAN'T BELIEVE you're actually doing this. You're getting freaking married, Lyssa." I squeeze her into the tightest hug ever, just before we enter the bridal shop.

"That's if I can find a dress. I can't believe I'm getting married tomorrow and I don't even have a dress."

"Please, that man would marry you even if you wore a paper bag." Sarah rolls her eyes.

"*Mmmhmm.* He would, wouldn't he? Let's hope it doesn't come to that," Lyssa says, pushing her way through the door with the rest of us following suit.

"Okay, here's what we are going to do. Each of us pick one dress and Lyssa you pick two that you really love, then you're going to try each dress on." When we all just stare at Sarah like she's lost her mind, she claps at us. "Chop, chop, girls, the day's a wasting."

We all go about finding our version of the perfect dress for Lyssa. I'm going through a rack with Ella beside me.

"So, do you think we'll be doing this again for you soon?" she asks.

I all but choke on thin air. "God, no," I get out, then notice her scrunched up face.

"Not that I don't love Bray, all that is Bray, but marriage is not something I need." I try to explain myself; it's not working too well.

"Does Bray know that? Because I'm pretty certain you are his forever, Reilly."

"I know. Trust me, Ella, he is my forever too. I just don't think you need to get married to be forever."

"Okay, I just don't want to see Bray get hurt. I know he comes across like nothing bothers him, but you have the ability to break him."

Wow, I admire how protective she is of him. I'm wondering if Lyssa got the same speech. Probably not.

"Ella, I promise I won't do anything to hurt your brother. Honestly, I've never loved anyone else as much as I love him. It's different, the feelings I have for Bray. It's consuming, like I can't even breathe properly when he's not around. And when he is around, well, I feel like a damn dog in heat, 'cause all I want to do is jump him. I want to crawl into his skin. It's like I can never get close enough, you know? I don't ever want to wake up without him next to me."

Ella screws her face up. "First, *eew*, I do not need to hear about you and Bray jumping anything. Second, you really do love him. I know that. I just worry more about him than I do Zac. Ever since our parents died, Bray has been a little lost and a lot angry. That's why he fights. Since meeting you, he has a newness about him and I worry what would happen to him if you weren't around anymore, that's all."

I get that, I do. "Never stop looking out for your brothers, Ella. Life is short and can change in the blink of an eye. They're both lucky to have an amazing sister like you. Now, how about we find that dress for Lyssa?" I suggest, changing the topic.

We go about choosing dresses, while I recall the things Holly and I would put the girls through who Dylan used to bring home. The year he died, he had only just started bringing girls around. We didn't get to torture him too much with our overprotectiveness.

"YOU KNOW, when I get married, I think I'll just fly to Vegas and elope," Ella says as we all sit on the couch waiting for Lyssa to come out of the changing room in her fourth dress. Sarah, Holly and I burst out laughing.

"Ella, hunny, if you ever fly to Vegas to get married, be sure to warn me so I can be around when Zac and Bray find out. Then change your name and go into witness protection with your new husband, because there is no way your brothers won't kill him, whoever he is," I tell her through my laughter.

"Please, the only way you're getting married is by running off to Vegas where those two buffoons can't protest against it," Sarah laughs. To which, I slap her arm, while at the same time Holly slaps her other one.

"*Ow*! What the fuck, Reilly?" she says, rubbing both of her arms.

"One of those buffoons happens to be mine, so you don't get to call him names without getting hurt." I smile at her.

"Well, what'd you slap me for, Holl? He's not your boyfriend." Holly shrugs her shoulders.

"Sorry, Sarah, but I knew Reilly was going to do it the minute the words left your lips, and I had this overwhelming urge to slap you too. It's her fault though, blame her," she says, pointing her finger at me.

"Thanks, Holl. Way to throw me under the bus." I blow her a kiss.

"Okay, this is the one, and I don't care what any of you say, I love it," Lyssa says as she walks out of the dressing room. She looks up and points a finger at Ella. "Don't you ever think about running off to Vegas. No sister of mine is having a Vegas elopement for a wedding."

Ella jumps up and hugs Lyssa. "You look gorgeous, Alyssa. Zac is going to blow a gasket when he sees you tomorrow."

"Thank you. So, what do you all think?" Lyssa asks the rest of us.

She looks absolutely stunning. "I love it," we all say at once.

"Perfect, this is it. Now we can go back and laze by the beach for the rest of the afternoon."

I HAVE a cocktail in hand and I'm lying on a sun lounger on a beach in Hawaii. Can life get any better than this? The sand is white, the water picture perfect and clear blue. It's like heaven, this place. I look over to Alyssa, who is wearing a tiny red bikini, her baby bump just starting to show. She's been drinking mock-tails all day and complaining about not being able to drink with us. Meanwhile, Ella has been sneaking sips of my drink all day, because she's not old enough to drink here.

"I can't wait to be an aunt. You know I'll be the favourite; you might as well go and name her Reilly already. Break the news early to the rest, Lyssa; let them down gently," I tell her.

She laughs, "Oh my God, you are spending way too much time with Bray!" She points at me. "That's exactly what he said to me the other day."

I smile thinking about spending even more time with Bray. "He told you to name her Reilly?"

"No, he said I should name him Bray, after his favourite uncle.".

"Well, Bray can take a number. I'm calling dibs. Besides, this baby is going to be a girl," I say around my straw, while eyeing the candy walking up the beach.

Putting my finger between my lips, I let out the loudest wolf whistle I can, gaining the attention of the hunks currently headed in our direction. Although my eyes are zoned in on only one of them.

He's wearing a pair of board shorts and nothing else; *mmm,* I lick my suddenly dry lips. My eyes follow the droplets of water travelling down his smooth, tanned skin, to those abs I want to sink my teeth into.

When my eyes finally make it back up to his, he gives me that panty-melting smirk. Yep, my bikini bottoms are now wet, and not just from the water of the ocean.

My favourite parts of Bray though, are those arms. They're strong, can hold me up like I weigh nothing, and are decorated with colourful tattoos. I want those arms wrapped around me. I want those hands all over me. I'm getting more and more heated by the minute. I'm going to need to go back into the water to cool off.

And then the idea hits me, yes. I'm going back out into that ocean, but I'm not going alone. As if he can read my mind, Bray looks back over his shoulder at the water then to me and smiles. He's way too tuned in to the way my mind works now.

Once they meet up with us, Zac heads straight for the towel basket. Picking one up, he places it over top of Alyssa like a bloody blanket, to which she throws it off.

"Sunshine, what if the baby gets sunburnt? You really should cover up." Alyssa glares at him and he eventually backs down, choosing to sit in front of her on her lounger while effectively blocking the view of her to anyone not in our little group.

It dawns on me that Bray has never once cared about what I wear, or tried to get me to not wear something revealing. It's odd, considering how against revealing clothing Zac is. I've seen how Bray will try to get Ella to change or refuse to let her leave the house until she does. But he's never done this with me.

He squats over top of me, practically straddling me while holding himself up as he leans in to kiss me. I pull back, to which he screws his face up and raises an eyebrow in question at me.

"Why do you never care about what I wear out in public?" I blurt out.

"Babe, you can wear whatever you like. You're fucking gorgeous in anything you wear anyway," he shrugs. "Plus, I can fight." He's so matter of fact.

"What does fighting have to do with how I look?" I ask, confused.

"Any fucker who wants to stare too long or try to touch what's mine will learn very quickly just how good I can fight, babe." Cocky fucking bastard, he is. Problem is it's bloody true, he can fight, and he is good at it.

Deciding I like his answer, I pull his face down to meet mine—his hand quickly going to my throat and holding me still. I try my hardest not to moan out loud, but he knows what it does to me when he grabs me by the throat; shivers wreak havoc through my body.

I push him away with my hands; let's face it, we all know he lets me push him away. "I want to go for a swim, and you're coming with me." I don't give him room to say no, not that he would. Before I know it, I'm tossed over his shoulder and he's jogging towards the water. I have to hold onto my bikini top to make sure my boobs don't jump out of the fabric.

Once he makes it to the water, I think he's going to

put me down, but no, he walks until he's waist-deep and throws me in. I come up coughing and spluttering.

"Asshole, I'm going to kill you," I scream at him, once I have my footing and my lung capacity back, that is.

He grabs and pulls me against him. "No, you're not. You love me way too much to do that," he says, so assured of himself.

"*Mmm*, you're right. I need to get a mould of junior made before I can do that. At least that way, junior and I can still have playdates without needing the rest of you." I smirk at him.

"Harsh, babe. That's fucking harsh. Your life would be boring as shit without me, admit it." He starts tickling my sides.

"No, Braydon Williamson, stop!" I scream, but no one is around to help me.

"I'll stop when you admit it," he says, continuing his torture.

"Okay, okay, my life would suck without you, happy?" I give in. Also, it's the bloody truth.

He stops. I jump up and wrap my legs around his waist and his lips meet mine in the softest, most tender kiss he has ever given me. Pulling back, I lose myself in the green orbs of his eyes.

"I want to remember this moment forever, trap it in a jar and keep it on the shelf," I tell him.

"No need, babe, we will have a lifetime of moments like these."

"Promise?"

"I will make sure of it. I'm never giving us up, Reilly." I need him inside me, now, more than ever before. Reaching down between our bodies, I undo his board shorts, just enough to free his cock. I move my bikini bottoms to the side and let his cock slide into my entrance.

"Fuck." He holds me still, buried onto him with my legs wrapped around his waist. To anyone looking, if they could even see through the water, we just look like two people holding each other.

He thrusts in and out, so tenderly and slow. It's the sweetest form of torture. We've never made love like this, each always too hungry for the other and going rough and hard. But this, I like this too.

"I love you more than I thought I could ever love anyone, Bray," I confess while he places gentle kisses all over my face.

"Your heart is safe in my hands, babe. I promise, no matter what life throws our way, you will always have me to lean on. I will always fight for us."

We spend the next thirty minutes making love in the waters of Waikiki Beach. I lock this moment into my memory of the time I knew one hundred percent, without a doubt, that I would spend the rest of my life with this man. The scary thought, if he asked me to run off and elope with him tomorrow, I'd probably say yes. I'll keep that thought to myself though—I do not need to encourage his crazy antics.

# CHAPTER EIGHTEEN

BRAY

*T*HESE LAST COUPLE of days in this paradise with Reilly have been amazing. I can't even remember the last time I was on any sort of vacation. It was before my parents died. Zac has never taken this much time off work for anything before. He would take time out to attend school events for Ella, or to drag my ass out of whatever trouble it found, but he'd always be straight back to working mode.

During Ella's younger years of high school, Zac never went into the club before Ella was asleep. He made sure he was home during the afternoon and evening with her. And when he went into the club, he had either me or Dean stay in the penthouse while she slept. I didn't mind though; I'd do anything for Ella.

Even though I was a shit of a kid when our parents died, I would have done whatever Zac needed me to do to help him and Ella. Family always came first.

Being on this week's wedding getaway has made me take note of how much we need to do this more as a family. Now that our little family of three is growing rapidly, with the baby on his way; and yes, I'm counting on getting a boy. We need to do this; that child needs to experience family holidays like we did as kids. I have no doubt Zac will ensure that he experiences everything life has to offer. He really is going to be a great dad.

"Bray, hurry up, you cannot be late to your own brother's wedding," James yells through the bathroom door. Why the fuck Zac thought he needed to bring the bartender along, I have no idea, something about him being one of Alyssa's people or some bullshit like that.

"James, bang on that door again and I'll bang your fucking head into it!" I yell back.

The fucker laughs. "What would Reilly say if you did that, Bray?"

Fuck, that little shit had to go and make besties with Reilly. Now I can't fucking touch him and he knows it. I can, however, still threaten him.

"She won't know if she never finds the body, and trust me, James, no one will ever find the body."

"Okay, okay, just hurry up. I am not taking on Zac's wrath when we show up late because you need to spend an hour in front of the mirror."

I'm hurrying already, anxious to get back in the same room as Reilly. She left early this morning, claiming they needed the whole day to glam. I tried to tell her she wakes up already full of glam, and she told me where to shove my sweet-talking mouth. I gladly spent the morning following her direction, because only an idiot would say no to getting their mouth on her pussy.

SITTING IN THE HOT SUN, on the white sand of Honolulu, I watch my brother stand on the alter waiting for Alyssa, every few seconds checking his watch. She's not late—he's just an impatient bastard. Reilly is sitting to my right, gripping my hand hard, excitement running through her. Ella is on my left; I can see tears already forming in her eyes.

I've never understood why people fucking cry at weddings; it's a happy occasion, or at least it should be. There's no need for tears. I watch as Zac suddenly stops fidgeting and his head snaps up, mouth hanging open. Looking behind me, I see Alyssa standing at the end of the aisle. She looks stunning, a long white dress waving in the wind.

There is just one problem—she's by herself. For some reason, this resonates with me. She should not be walking down the aisle by herself. Call me sappy but every girl should have somebody to walk them down the aisle on their wedding day. I know, I'm a fucking hopeless romantic at heart.

I jump up and everyone looks in my direction. I don't fucking care. Reilly tries to pull me back down, but I wink at her. "I gotta do something. Wait here." I jog down the aisle, stopping in front of Alyssa.

She looks up at me confused. "You look beautiful, Lyssa," I tell her.

"*Ahh*, thanks, Bray," she says, eyebrows drawn.

"I thought you could use my arm to lean on, while you walk down this long-ass aisle. You know, so you don't break an ankle in your heels." I hold my arm out. I can see the tears immediately form in her eyes.

"Don't you dare fucking cry on me, woman. If I make you cry on your wedding day, Zac really will kill me."

She takes a big breath in. "Okay, thank you, Bray. I really appreciate you doing this."

"You're my sister. I'd do anything for you."

Alyssa grabs my arm and we begin our walk back down the aisle. She leans in and whispers, "I know you can see that I'm wearing sandals and not heels, by the way." She holds my arm tighter.

"I know." I smile at her. We get to the end, and I take her hand and place it in Zac's. That fucker is about to bawl his eyes out too. Am I the only one around here who's not about to cry like a fucking baby? Zac gives me a head nod, and I turn and make my way to a sniffling Reilly and Ella. *God, help me.*

The minister starts the ceremony. A lot of it, I tune out until it's time for the vows. They're really the only part that actually matter, right? I think when I convince Reilly to marry me, we will skip all the other shite and get right down to business on those vows. I can hear the emotion in Zac's voice as he reads out his vows.

Zac starts, "Alyssa, you came into my life like a ray of sunshine on a rainy day. You are the most caring, compassionate and kind-hearted person I know. I'm truly humbled that you have chosen me to share your life with. I promise to work every day to be the man that deserves your love. I promise to love you with every fibre of my being. I promise to never let you walk alone, to always be by your side. Sunshine, you are my first, my last, my everything and I promise to be yours for as long as you'll have me. I vow to always be your friend, your lover, and most importantly your family, for now until forever—it's you and me Alyssa, merged as one. I promise we will always have tomorrow together."

Alyssa continues, "Zac, I never dreamed of finding someone like you, ever. I've never known the kind of love and devotion you have given me. I've never had a family to call my own. Because of you, I can say that I am truly loved. Because of you, I can say that I have a family. Because you're by my side, always, I know I can conquer anything. You are the love I thought only existed in books; you are my hero, Zac. You are my home, my safe place and my happy ending. I have seen the best of you and the worst of you, and I choose both. I promise to love and cherish you always. I promise to be your sunshine on the darkest of days. I vow that our love will merge us together throughout all of time. I promise to always be your tomorrow."

"You may kiss the bride," the minister declares, and everyone around me cheers. Reilly looks over at my silent face.

"Bray? Are you crying?" she whispers. I love her even more for not calling me out in front of everyone.

"I'm not crying, just something got caught in my eye." I try to play it off like Zac and Alyssa's vows did not choke me up.

"*Uh-huh*, sure. Don't worry, your secret is safe with me." She leans up and kisses me.

"I think we should get married," I tell her.

"Sure, one day. But today, let's celebrate Zac and Alyssa," she says, standing and pulling me along with her.

It doesn't hit me until hours later that she agreed to

get married, that she didn't say no. She said *sure, one day* to me and that's as good as a yes. I plan on asking her properly though, maybe even pay her dad a visit and do this the old fashion way. Not that his disapproval would stop me from marrying her.

THE REST of the week flew by—I had Reilly, the beach and an endless supply of food and alcohol. I could not have wanted for anything else. The flight home however was painful as fuck. Alyssa spent half of the flight with her head in the toilet, throwing up. It seems the morning sickness has kicked in for her.

Zac spent the whole flight stressing out and cursing at everyone. He went as far as to demand the pilot have an ambulance on standby the minute we land. Alyssa vetoed that idea quickly. Zac was pissed. I kind of got it. He felt helpless and he couldn't do much to help her. It's also his own damn fault she's in this position, which I gladly reminded him of every chance I got.

We flew in late last night and I ended up staying at Reilly's place. Waking to a cooked breakfast by Reilly's mum is something I would never turn down. I tried to convince Lynne to move in with me, but she laughed it off like I was joking. I'm not fucking joking—I'd build that woman her own wing if she cooked for me like this.

After eating a shit load of pancakes, bacon and eggs, I head to the gym—probably to get blasted by coach for laxing off so much the last week—dropping Reilly off at the club on my way.

Halfway through training, my phone started blaring Reilly's ring tone. Climbing out of the cage, I grab the phone off the bench.

"Hey, babe, what's up?" I ask, breathlessly.

"Bray, I don't know what to do," she whispers down the phone. Something is wrong. I pick my keys up and run out of the gym.

"Reilly, what's wrong?" I'm opening the door to my car, but what she tells me stops me momentarily.

"There's a guy here pointing a gun around. He's on the ground floor."

Fuck. "Reilly, can you get to the lift?"

"Yes, I'm on the top floor. He doesn't know I'm here." "Good, get in the lift, put the code in for the basement.

Once the basement code is entered, the lift won't stop. Stay in the basement until I come and get you. Do not leave that basement, Reilly. Promise me."

"Okay, I promise, I won't leave the basement."

"Good, stay on the phone until it cuts out. Once you're in the lift, the reception will die. I'm coming for you, babe."

I stay on the line. I hear her enter the code and the elevator start its downward journey, then the line cuts off. Fuck. What the fuck. I dial Zac, no answer. I dial Dean, no answer. I just need to get to the club; once I'm there, I can figure the fuck out what to do about this shit show.

I WALK in through the back doors quietly. I have no idea what the fuck I'm walking into. I can hear it before I see it. "Call your fucking pussy-ass brother down here now, before I start dropping cunts," the voice yells. I know I've heard that voice before, I can't place it though.

When I see what's happening, I freeze. Zac has a gun pointed to his fucking head.

"You're going to have to shoot me, motherfucker, because if you think I'm putting my brother in front of your crazy ass, think again."

I'm about to walk out, then the front doors to the club open and my heart sinks. She's meant to be in the fucking basement. Why the fuck would she waltz through the front doors? Then it clicks—it's not Reilly… it's Holly.

Fuck. The guy with the gun, who I now know is that fucking singer from Cyrus, turns and points the gun at Holly.

"Well, well, well. If everyone else here isn't enough to get him out here, maybe his hot little girlfriend here will be."

Holly freezes, dropping everything in her hands. I can see her body shaking. I walk out from the shadows. I will not let anyone else take a bullet that's got my name on it.

"I'm right here, motherfucker. What the fuck are you gonna do about it?" I yell out, getting his attention off Holly, the gun now firmly pointing at me. I can see Dean in the background, creeping up behind him and placing himself in front of Holly, thank fuck. Zac curses.

"You know, I wanted to shoot you. I came here to kill you. I know you assholes had something to do with my brother going missing. I know you did."

"It was me. I choked the life out of him after I cut every one of his fucking fingers off with garden sheers.

But if you want to blame someone for your rapist, woman-beating brother being dead, blame him. He attacked my fucking eighteen-year-old sister. He deserved every fucking bit of torture I dished out and then some," Zac growls as he moves closer to me.

"You know what? I have to live without my brother. Now you're going to find out what that's like." The asshole points the gun back at me and pulls the trigger.

I see Dean tackle him to the ground. *A bit fucking late, Dean.* I look at Zac, and his face is ashen. I look him up and down; he's in one piece and I thank God right before I fall to the ground. Zac's screaming. I can't make out the words, but I see his lips moving. He's got his hands over my chest. I can feel a burning, searing pain ripping through me. I go to my happy place and think of Reilly. I smile. Reilly is safe. She's the last thing I think of before I black out.

# CHAPTER NINETEEN

REILLY

*I* KNOW I promised Bray I'd stay in the basement—I should stay in the basement—but something twists in my gut. Something is wrong with Holly. I can feel it. I can't name what it is, but I feel fear like I've never felt before. Bone crunching coldness runs through my veins. My skin is prickling, sweat running down my spine.

Shit, Holly is here; she was bringing me lunch today. There is currently a mad gunman waving a fucking gun around on the ground floor and my sister's going to walk through those doors, or probably already has.

Sorry, Bray, but I can't just sit here. I have to do something.

I punch the code into the lift that will let me out near the back of the ground floor. The trip back up from the basement feels like it takes forever. Just as the doors open, I hear a gunshot. Loud ringing rages through my ears. I know, I'm the idiot in all the horror films that runs towards the bad guy, but instinct takes over and run I do, out towards the middle of the ground floor.

I can hear Zac shouting, and Dean fighting someone on the floor. I see Holly standing at the door-way, intact, thank God. She makes eye contact with me, her eyes filled with an expression I've only ever seen once before, when our brother died. An overwhelming sadness blankets her, tears running down her face.

I can still hear Zac shouting, and when I look in his direction, my whole world falls apart. I feel like the rug has literally been pulled from under my feet. I can't move. I can't breathe. Why can't I breathe? As I struggle for oxygen, I fall to the ground on my hands and knees. A scream retches its way from my throat, but I don't hear it. The room is spinning in silence. Someone touches my arm. James. I look up at him. He is talking but I don't hear a word of what he's saying.

I need to get to him. I have to get to him. I drag myself up and run, stumbling to Bray. Bray, who is laid out on the floor, blood covering the front of his body and spilling out beside him. Falling to my knees next to him, I look up to Zac, who has his hands over the gaping wound in his chest.

"Zac, wh… what do I do? Tell me what to do," I cry, wanting to do something but not knowing what to do. "Where the fuck is the ambulance? Somebody, get a fucking ambulance here now!" Zac yells out.

"They're two minutes away. Keep pressure on the wound," James says from behind me.

I lean down next to Bray's face and whisper in his ear, "Don't you dare fucking leave me, Braydon Williamson, not when I've just found you." I'm a slobbering mess.

Holly comes and sits next to me; she grabs my hand and holds on tight. My other hand grasps Bray's. Why does he feel so lifeless? Cold? Where the hell is the ambulance? One minute later, I'm being shoved out of the way by ambulance officers. I refuse to let go of Bray's hand; he needs me. I need to help him. Zac ends up picking me up off the floor and moving me out of the way.

"Reilly, we have to let them help him. They have to help him," he says to me.

I watch as the medics work on the other half of my soul. I watch as they place his lifeless body on the gurney and wheel him out to the ambulance on the street, all the while continuing to work on him. I watch, totally helpless to do anything to save the man I love.

"Let's go," Zac says, dragging me by the hand out of the club. He puts me in the car before running around to the driver's seat and flying out to catch up to the ambulance that just took off. The whole trip Zac manages to stay directly behind the ambulance, not bothering to stop at red lights, screeching around street corners, and ducking in and out of the busy Sydney city traffic.

"I can't lose him. I can't lose him. I only just found him," I repeat over and over.

"We are not losing him, Reilly. It's not a fucking option," Zac yells at me. His hands clench the steering wheel.

As soon as he stops at the emergency room doors, I jump out of the car. The drive has allowed time for some of my shock to wear off. I run through the emergency room, stopping at the counter. I can see Bray being wheeled in by the paramedics through the plexiglass of the triage counter.

There are doctors and nurses rushing in every direction, calling out words I don't understand. Then I spot Alyssa; she's standing there staring at Bray. Her head pops up at something a doctor says and I hear her yell at them, "This is my fucking brother! You do everything you can. Now!"

Another nurse grabs her by the arm and pulls her away from the gurney as they wheel it to another room. By this time, Zac is standing next to me watching the same scene.

"Get your fucking hands off my wife before I cut them off," he growls through the plexiglass window. This makes Alyssa turn and notice us. She runs out the door and straight into Zac's arms, allowing herself only a moment of comfort, before she stands back and looks between us. We are both covered in blood, Bray's blood.

"What happened?" she asks quietly.

I don't even know what to tell her. I go to speak; my mouth opens but no words come out. I can't get the words to work. The panic is creeping up on me. I can feel my skin getting hot, my breathing becoming more and more difficult as I gulp to drag air into my lungs. My hands clutch at my throat, and I bend at the waist, trying to breathe, trying to just count to ten.

Zac grabs my face in his hands. He bends down to my level. "Reilly, fucking breathe. I am not going to be telling my brother that his girlfriend stopped breathing when he comes out of that theatre room." I search his eyes for the lie, that Bray's not coming out of that room. I can't see it, the lie; it's not there. He believes that Bray is coming out of this.

"Reilly, I need you to have more faith in him. Don't you dare fucking give up on him," he tells me.

I nod my head in agreement, but I feel him slipping away already. I feel a loss like no other, like a part of me has died, burnt, and is now ashes blowing in the wind. A part of me that I will never get back.

"I'm going to go back and see if I can find anything out," Alyssa says.

"Wait, why are you even here, sunshine? You told me you quit this job weeks ago," Zac questions.

"I tried to call you to tell you I was coming in. I got called; they were short-staffed and desperate. It's just for the day." She leans up and kisses him.

"I don't care how much money I have to throw at this fucking hospital, make sure he has the best doctors in that theatre room," Zac tells her. Alyssa nods her head, before walking back through the doors, leaving Zac and me standing in the waiting room—both unsure of what to do now.

FOUR HOURS LATER, I'm seated on the horrible plastic chairs, cuddled into Holly. Ella is clinging onto Dean like a lifeline, silent tears streaming down her face. Alyssa and Sarah are sitting opposite Holly and me, both quiet.

Zac hasn't stopped pacing the room; up and down, he keeps moving. A few times Alyssa has tried to get him to sit down, but he won't. The only times he stops pacing is when she throws herself into his arms and he clings to her, whispering in her ear.

I hate this waiting. Why hasn't someone been out here already? What's taking so bloody long? With each minute that passes, any little hope I have dwindles away. Pretty soon, I'm going to be all out of hope. I'm going to be left with nothing, left to pick up the pieces of a broken heart again. Except this time, it's not just broken, it's shattered into a million pieces.

A doctor walks out and calls out, "Family of Braydon Williamson."

"That's me," Zac and I both say at the same time. I jump out of my chair and rush up to the doctor. Ella comes up and stands quietly next to Zac.

"He looks between the both of us. And you are his..." He leaves the question open.

I look to Zac for an answer. If I say I'm his girl-friend, they are not letting me through. I know the drill.

"I'm his brother; this is his sister." He points to Ella. Then he looks over to me. "This is his wife Reilly." Zac's lie slips out of his mouth effortlessly.

For once in my life, I actually wish it weren't a lie. I wish I was Bray's wife. Why didn't I marry him weeks ago when he wanted to fly to Vegas? The next time he asks if we can fly to Vegas, I'm jumping on that. Please God, let there be a next time.

"Okay, Braydon suffered a gunshot wound to his abdomen. The bullet tore through his small intestine.

We had to remove part of the bowel. He also suffered from a dangerous level of blood loss. He's stable for now and is in the ICU. He is in a medically-induced coma for the time being. I can take the two of you back to see him for a few minutes, but you'll have to wait until we move him to a private room for any longer visitations."

All I heard was he is stable. He's okay... he's going to be okay. I haven't lost him yet. My hope wants to climb back up from the ashes, but I need to see him first.

Zac grabs my hands and holds on tight. "Thank you," he says to the doctor. We follow the doctor down long corridors until we finally make it to a ward that reads ICU on top of the doors. Zac squeezes my hand tighter. "He's going to be okay," he whispers. I'm not sure if he's trying to reassure me or himself.

When we make it into the ward, the doctor stops at a curtained-off section. There is a nurse doing something with buttons on machines that persistently beep. I listen to the beeps, taking comfort in the beat of his heart playing out through the machine. Letting go of Zac's hand, I slowly make my way to Bray's side. He looks peaceful, even with all the tubes and cords attached to him everywhere, he looks peaceful.

I gently hold his hand. "Bray, I need you to keep fighting for me. Just hold on that little bit longer and come back to me. Please, don't you dare let go," I whisper to him.

Zac wraps his arm around my shoulder. "He's a fighter, Reilly, and there's never been a fight he hasn't won. Trust me, he's not giving up." Zac lets go of me, turns to the doctor, and asks, "When is he being moved to a private room? And when will he be woken up?"

"He'll be moved up in a few hours. As for waking him up, we will slowly bring him out of the induced coma starting tomorrow. Sometimes it takes hours, sometimes a day. It all depends on his body. He's not out of the woods yet. The next twenty-four hours are critical to telling us how his recovery will be," the doctor replies.

"Good, I want him in the best room you have. Money is not an object," Zac states like it's a done deal, like money will fix everything.

Money does not fix everything. Money could not save my brother. Money could not keep my dad out of jail. And no amount of money will save Bray. I know that, and deep down, Zac knows that too. Bray's recovery is out of our hands, all we can do is sit back and hope. But hoping has never worked in my favour before.

"It's been two fucking days. Why the fuck is he not waking up?" Zac growls at the doctor, who is currently trying to do his rounds.

"These things take time. The drugs have worked their way out of his system. The only thing keeping him asleep is his own body not being ready to wake up. His brain activity scans are normal, and there is no sign of damage. All we can do is wait," the doctor responds calmly.

"Wait, how long do we have to wait?"

"Zac, hunny. The doctors can't answer that; you know that. We just have to be patient, and let them do their jobs. He will wake up. He has to," Alyssa says, pulling Zac out of the doctor's way.

Zac doesn't reply. He wraps his arms around Alyssa and stares at what the doctors are doing, watching their every move, like he's waiting to pounce on someone.

Me? I'm sitting in the same place I've been for the past two days, in the uncomfortable chair by Bray's bed. Holly has been bringing me changes of clothes. I use the private bathroom Bray has, taking less than five minutes to shower and change. I can't risk him waking up and me not being there. I need to be there when he wakes up. The couple of times I have showered, I made sure Holly took my place. At least then if he woke up, he would still see me, or a very close second.

# CHAPTER TWENTY

*Bray*

𝓘 CAN SMELL the fruity scent all around me. I smile—that's Reilly. That's my girl's fucking delicious smell. I don't know where I am. I feel like I'm floating, but I can't see anything around me, surrounded only by a whiteness. I keep getting to this spot. I can hear voices. I can smell, but I can't make anything else out, no matter how much I try.

She's here though. I can feel her presence surrounding me. Reilly is here with me. I just need to find her. I hear her voice like a musical melody calling to me, reaching for me, but I'm trapped in this whiteness.

"Bray, you can wake up now. It's been a week. Stop being a lazy ass and get up. What would your coach say when he hears you've been asleep for a week?"

*Coach would rip me a new one*, I want to reply, except she never hears me.

"Bray, please, you promised me. You promised that you would always fight for us. I'm begging you to fight your way back for us."

Her cries rip through my heart. I want to hold her, to tell her that I'm fucking fighting. I'm fighting to get back to her. I just need to find her. *Where are you, baby?*

I can feel myself slip back to darkness, to nothingness. The sounds around me, the beeping, the talking, it all fades out.

I'M BACK in the whiteness. I inhale, hoping to get a whiff of that fruity fragrance. It's not there. She's not here. I want to let myself slip back into the darkness, then I hear Ella.

"Bray, I moved into my dorm at the university. You were meant to help me, you know. You were meant to do all the heavy lifting for me. I had to take Zac and

Dean—guess how that turned out? Zac decided that the dorm room was unacceptable accommodations. His exact words. I never knew how much of a snob our big brother was. Dean agreed, saying the security was not high enough. It's a bloody girls' dorm room, Bray. What the hell do I need security for there?"

I'm hoping that Zac ended up refusing her move into the dorms. Like I originally did. I knew those dorms would suck. I may not have gone to university, but I spent many days in the girls' dorms when I was younger.

"Do you know what Zac went and did next? No, you don't know because you won't wake up. He went and bought an apartment near the university and said if I had to move out, that was the only option. So, now I have a not so little two-bedroom apartment, five minutes away from the university. No sharing a tiny dorm room with a stranger for me. I gave him hell for it though. I'm not admitting that I love that apartment way more than a dorm room. And if you wake up and tell him I said that, I'll knock you over the head and put you back to sleep."

Thank the Lord she is not in those dorm rooms. I can't believe Zac had to be showy and buy her an apartment. I would have talked her into moving in with me if she didn't want to continue living with Zac.

"Bray, wake the fuck up already. It's been three weeks." It's Zac; he sounds pissed, which is nothing new. I'm used to him being pissed at me.

"Bray, I can't do everything without you. You need to wake up. If not for me, do it for Reilly then. That poor girl has not left this hospital for weeks. She won't leave your room for any longer than five minutes at a time. You can't do this to her. You can't do this to me, fucker. You don't get to just sleep while the rest of us are here suffering and worried."

I'm fucking trying. I want to get back to Reilly. I want to hold her in my arms more than anything. If I can just find the way. How the fuck do I wake up?

"Bray, you promised me that you were great uncle material. Being asleep is not being a great uncle. Wake up. Your nephew needs an uncle who can teach him how to fight and how to get all the ladies. That's right. I said nephew; we found out it was a boy. Although, if he takes after his father, he won't need any help. That man is so skilled. The stories I could tell you. And if you don't wake up soon, I might just start spilling my guts and torture you with the horrid details of your brother's and my sex life, amazing bloody sex life. I know you can hear me, Braydon Williamson. Wake the hell up."

Fuck, pregnancy has made Alyssa grouchy. Where the fuck is Reilly? I can't smell her fragrance. All I want is Reilly.

"BRAY, I'm falling apart. I don't know what to do."
*Mmm*, I can smell that fruity fragrance. Reilly is here.
She sounds so fucking lost though. How can I reassure
her that I'm still here? No matter what I do, I can't
seem to pull myself out of this, whatever the fuck
this is.

"You said you would fight. You promised I would
never be alone again. Well, I'm feeling pretty bloody
lonely right now, Bray. Please wake up. I will do
anything. You want to run off to Vegas and get
married? Let's do it. Just wake up, please."

Please, God, let me remember that when I eventually make it out of this fog. Let me hold her to that
promise of marriage.

"Please," she sobs. I can hear her cries and can't do a
damn thing about it. As much as I try to tell my body
I'm ready to get this show on the road, nothing
happens. The darkness just keeps taking over me again
and again.

# CHAPTER TWENTY-ONE

*Reilly*

𝓘'M WATCHING the useless bloody doctors do their observations on Bray again. It's been the same thing, day in and day out, for the last fifty-nine days. They can't find anything wrong with his brain; they don't know why he isn't waking up.

Zac has called in the best neurologists he can find. He's flown doctors in from all over the place. All of them unable to give us any answers. As much as my hope has dwindled, I can't give up. He made me a promise to always fight for us, so that is what I have resolved to do. Fight, for me, for him, for us.

I spend my days sitting by his side, researching patients suffering from comas. I have tried every single damn method I can find on the internet aimed at waking up coma patients. I've been playing his favourite songs. I've replayed videos of his own fights. I even made his coach come in and yell at him, ordering him to wake up. As much as he didn't want to do it, I was not going to take no for an answer.

It didn't work though—nothing worked. I'm running out of ideas. I don't want to give up, I can't give up, but I really don't know what to do. Zac and Ella spend hours here every day too. I have been leaving them to have their own time with Bray.

I wanted to make sure I was the person he saw when he woke up. He told me once that the first thing he wanted to see in the mornings was my face; the second my *friendly vagina,* his words, because that was the best way to start the day. I replied that coffee was the best start to the day. I wish I had told him that wasn't true. I should have told him that he was the best start to every day… the best end to every day.

Now, I'm scared that when he wakes up—if he wakes up… no, it's when he wakes up—I'm terrified he's not going to know who I am. I was only in his life for a few months. Maybe it should be Zac or Ella whom he sees first; they're his family. What do I do if he doesn't remember me?

He fell in love with me once, and that was when I was trying to push him away. I can get him to fall in love with me again. I think. Maybe. Hopefully. It's only been a few months, but I don't even know who I am without Bray anymore.

Actually, I do. That's a lie. Without Bray, I will go

back to the closed-off, frightened girl I was before. I will go back to being surrounded by people but feeling a bone-deep loneliness. I'll go back to being the fun Reilly, who to outsiders doesn't have a care in the world, while silently dying on the inside.

I can feel myself getting more and more frustrated at the doctors. They walk around looking at this and that, but they can't fix him. I want to yell and throw stuff. I want to stomp my foot and throw a tantrum, to demand they wake him up. I know that won't work though. Zac has already tried. Bray's scans have shown that his brain is responding to hearing our voices. Alyssa says we should keep touching him and keep talking to him, because he can hear everything we say. So, I've been doing just that. I have told him every-thing, my whole life story, almost.

I haven't told him about Dylan. He knows that I had a brother. He knows that he died obviously; he's been taking me to the jail and cemetery on the first Sunday of the month. He *was* taking me, when he was awake. Twice, he made up an excuse that he needed to visit his friend, who was in the same jail as my dad—his visits always the same time that I would be going there. He would then drive me to the cemetery, without me even asking; he would pull up and then lean against the car for an hour waiting on me, while I spent an hour talking to Dylan.

Bray never complained about waiting so long, and he never asked questions about my visits. Not because he wasn't interested—I knew he wanted to know. He was just waiting for me to be ready to talk about it. But that's the thing, I didn't think I'd ever be ready. There is so much anger, sadness and regret that I have over Dylan's death.

I wait for the doctors and nurses to leave the room, then climb up on the bed and cuddle into Bray. I don't care that I keep getting told off by the nursing staff. He's my boyfriend; if I want to lay in bed with him, I bloody will. One nurse made the mistake of telling me off for doing this while Zac was in the room. Well, let's just say that nurse left in tears.

Zac and I have gotten closer over the last two months. He has been caring and compassionate towards me like never before. It was a little odd at first, since we loved to hate each other, not that we ever actually hated each other. Now, he treats me just the same as he treats Ella and Alyssa. He is constantly asking if I need anything, constantly having food sent to me here at the hospital. Holly even told me he tried to give her that fancy black card of his to go and buy me clothing, toiletries and whatever other *woman crap* I need.

She laughed at him and said we didn't need his fancy money. Which I don't. We both have a nice little trust fund that our dad made sure we received when we turned twenty-one. Alyssa and Sarah know about this, but we don't tend to advertise it. I don't even think Holly has ever touched hers. I went through a phase where I was spending like I was Ariana Grande, then I woke up to myself and stopped.

Zac has also continued to pay me from the club, even though I haven't stepped foot in there since that day. I've told him he doesn't need to, that I don't deserve it. He grunts at me and tells me he's paying it anyway and not to bother arguing with him about it because I won't win.

Once we get out of this hospital, I plan on giving it all back, somehow. Even if I have to withdraw it all and dump a money bag in his mailbox, he is getting that money back. I am not now, nor have I ever been, a charity case. I just haven't had the energy to argue over it yet.

Curling up to Bray's side, I embrace the peace, all but the beeps of the machines. Everyone left a little while ago. These are the times I like the most, being able to curl up next to Bray. To touch him, feel that he is still here. To talk to him and tell him everything I can possibly think of.

The other day, I told him about the time when Holly and I were thirteen. There was a boy, we were playing seven minutes in heaven, and the bottle landed on Holly. She was expected to go into a closet with the boy I had a major crush on. There was no way Holl would kiss a boy I liked. We had completely different tastes in boys. Plus, there's the whole sister girl code thing. We went into the bathroom and changed clothes, came back out and I went into the closet with my crush. That was my first kiss, and it was absolutely horrible.

When I told him that story, I could have sworn I felt his hand move. I called for the nurse and she said it was probably just an involuntary twitch. I don't believe her. I got him to react I know it. I've felt these little twitches more and more lately. They can't be nothing. I won't believe that.

Taking a big breath in, I inhale his cologne. I've been spraying it on the pillows, on him, on the blankets. Just so I can surround myself in his scent. It's oddly comforting.

"Bray, you can wake up now. Everyone's gone home for the night so, you know, if you wanted to get laid, now's your chance, babe."

I grab hold of his hand. I could have sworn it twitched just then. Sometimes I'm convinced that I want it so bad that I'm imagining it.

"You can't leave me here, Bray. I still want you. I need you. I need you to wake up. You can't leave me. My dad left. Dylan left. I will not let you leave me. You know I never told you this, but when Dylan died, I thought I would never feel a pain so deep. I was wrong, because this, this right here, fucking hurts. It hurts that you're not keeping up to your end of the bargain and fighting for us. You're meant to be the undefeated fighter, Bray. Well, guess what, this, whatever this is, it's winning and you're losing. I'm losing."

I swipe the traitorous tears from my cheeks, take big breaths, and count to five before continuing.

"You want to know what I talk to Dylan about on those Sundays I visit him? Lately it's been about you. I tell him about everything that's been happening in my life. I tell him about Holly and my mum and dad. The first time you took me there, I asked him to give me a sign that you were the one I should take a chance on. That you were the one I should open my heart to. That same day, during the visit with my dad, he told me to give you a chance, to give happiness a chance. My dad had never led me wrong before, so I took a leap of faith."

Great, now my eyes are going to be red and blotchy again. I roll over and grab a tissue off the table before settling back in.

"I haven't been to see him, either of them, since you've been asleep. I can't bring myself to leave here, to leave you. If I could talk to Dylan right now, I'd tell him that my heart is shattered... that as much as I want to believe you're going to wake up and come back to me, I'm so freaking scared that you're not. Damn it, Bray, come back to me, please. I can't do this anymore. I'm tired; it's my turn to sleep. You need to wake up. I'm drowning right now and you don't even know. If you don't wake up, Bray, if you don't come back to me, then I'm likely to do something selfish and stupid and follow you. Because living like this, living without you, is not an option for me. I can't do it. I'm not that strong."

Movement of the hand I'm holding makes my whole body freeze. Did I imagine that? I wait and wait. A couple of minutes later that movement is there again. His fingers are curling—that's definitely more than a twitch. I want to look up, to look at his face, to see if his eyes are open. I'd do anything to be able to be entranced by those green eyes.

"*Rrh.*"

My head snaps up at the noise, and I jump off the bed. "Thank you, God. Thank you. Thank you. Thank you." They are there; the eyes, they're open. He's staring up at me, with very open eyes.

"Bray, don't move. Let me get someone."

Shit, what do I do? I don't know what I'm supposed to do. I look around the room in a panic; his curling fingers catch my attention. I'm still holding his hand. The pressure is light, featherlight. It's enough to let me know that he's there though, and that's all that matters.

Okay, think, Reilly. The call button, I press the call button, over and over and over again. It seems to take hours for the nurse to appear in the doorway.

"What on earth…" The nurse stops, mid-sentence, mid-stride. She only takes a minute to recover.

"Mr. Williamson, it's good to see you're awake," she says as she calmly walks over to the bed and presses some buttons on the machines. She then picks up the phone and informs whoever picks up that Bray is awake.

"You've given your wife quite the scare, Mr.

Williamson," the nurse says, patting my arm. She moves to the other side of the bed. Bray continues to stare up at me, confusion shining in his eyes.

He doesn't remember me. All I can think right now is he has no idea who I am. He's just woken up in hospital after being in a coma for two months and the first person he sees is practically a stranger. My eyes start welling up. I can feel his fingers applying pressure; they are attempting to curl around mine. I slip my hand out of his, look up to the nurse and excuse myself.

"*Umm*, I'm just going to step out into the hall and call

his brother. He should be here," I say as I leave. The nurse offers me a sympathetic look. I look back at Bray. He's actually awake. He's still staring straight at me.

Closing the door behind me, I lean against it, only to jump out of the way when a heap of doctors come down the hallway and enter the room. I should be in there. I should at least hear what's going on. First, I need to call Zac.

He picks up on the first ring. "Reilly, what's wrong? I'm coming now." I can hear the rustling of keys.

"Zac, he's awake."

"Wh... what did you say?" he whispers.

"Bray... he's awake. He just woke up a couple of minutes ago. You should get here, Zac. He's going to need you."

"I'm on my way. I'll be there in fifteen minutes. Are the doctors in with him?"

"Yes, they just went in." I don't know what to say. I don't know what to do. I've dreamt of this moment for two months, and now that it's here, I just don't know what I'm meant to do.

There's a loud commotion coming from Bray's room. What the hell? The nurse sticks her head out. "Mrs. Williamson, you need to get back in here, now."

Running into the room, I can hear the machine that's hooked up to Bray's heartbeat going haywire. "What's going on?" I ask as I barge my way through doctors to reach the other side of Bray's bed, the one not currently taken up by nurses and doctors.

I grab his hand in mine and watch as he turns his head towards me. His eyes lock onto mine. The machine starts to slow down. The doctors still and look up at me. I can see everyone looking at me, but I don't dare break eye contact with Bray.

"What happened?" I ask, still not looking away from Bray.

"It seems Mr. Williamson had what could be a slight panic attack. It started as soon as you left the room."

I scrunch my eyes up. Bray has never been scared of anything. Why the hell would he have a panic attack now?

# CHAPTER TWENTY-TWO

BRAY

SHE'S CRYING. I can feel her body heave with sobs. She's telling me about her brother, begging me to wake up. I'm trying to tell her that I am awake. My eyes are flickering open, adjusting to the brightness of the lights above me. This is the most alert and aware I have ever been. I'm not about to let the darkness pull me back under.

Reilly is telling me how broken she is, how much she needs me to wake up. Why can't I wake up? I'm trying to get my body to move anything. My fingers, I can feel them slightly move. What the fuck is wrong with me? What the fuck happened? And, why the fuck is Reilly sobbing right now?

I should be able to comfort her. I hate that she's upset and I can't do a damn thing to help her. It's my job to help her, to be her shoulder to cry on. I promised her I was going to be the best fucking boyfriend that ever existed and right now, I'm failing her.

I put everything into making my fingers move; they curl the slightest bit and I feel her body stiffen. Just look up, baby, just look up and you will see that I'm here. I'm awake. You told me to wake up and I listened. Just fucking look up already.

My brain is telling my mouth to speak. I can feel the words on the tip of my tongue, yet I'm getting nothing. What the fuck? I want to scream. I want to hit something, anything. Reilly, all I want to say is Reilly. Why the fuck can't I say the one name I fucking love so much?

After a few minutes of trying, I finally make a noise. I wouldn't call it talking, but it's noise and it gets her attention. Like lightening, she jumps off the bed and looks down. Her eyes widen and she starts speaking but I can't actually make out what she says. She's going too fast.

She's panicked. I curl my fingers. I try as hard as I can to squeeze her hand. She looks back down at me and seems to settle. Reaching over, she presses something behind my head. I just stare and watch. She's so fucking beautiful to look at, why wouldn't I stare? She doesn't look as vibrant as I remember; she's thinner, paler. She has black rings under her eyes, red puffy eyes, because she's been crying.

My thoughts are interrupted when someone comes barging into the room.

"What the hell..." Whoever this is, she stops for a second. It takes her no longer than a minute to recompose herself.

"Mr. Williamson, it's good to see you awake." She looks me over from head to toe.

I watch Reilly as she watches what must be a nurse pick up the phone. The nurse hangs up the call then pats Reilly on the arm. "You've given your wife quite the scare, Mr. Williamson," she says to me and looks over at Reilly.

Mrs. Williamson, who the fuck is Mrs. Williamson? Surely if I married Reilly that would not be something I'd forget. I certainly wouldn't be opposed to being married to her. In fact, if we are married, I'd make her marry me again so I can remember that shit. What else am I forgetting if I don't remember an important event like that?

Reilly still looks sad. Why is she still so sad? She excuses herself to the nurse, and says something about calling my brother. Zac, where is he? How long have I been asleep for? Reilly starts walking out of the room. I watch her the whole way. The moment she shuts the door and I can't see her anymore, I start to panic. I need her to come back. I need her to be here. I can't even fucking move. Why'd she walk out? Is she coming back?

The door opens, and I'm about to breathe a sigh of relief that she's back. It's not her; it's a heap of fuckers whom I don't know. Why would she leave me in here with all these people? The beeping starts to get louder and faster. I can feel my heartbeat match the sounds of the machine. I don't want to be here. Get me the fuck out of here.

Reilly comes running back into the room; she pushes her way through the people. People I'm cataloguing to kick their asses for blocking my girl's way. If I could get out of this bed, they would not be standing in her fucking way.

When she makes it to my side, she picks up my hand. I have to turn my head in the other direction, which, by some small miracle, it turns slightly and my eyes are focused back onto hers. I don't dare lose that eye contact. I don't want her to leave again. I can feel my heart start to calm. It's because she's here; she's my calm, my person. I fucking need her to stay here.

I listen as the doctors talk to her about me. They run a heap of tests. One of the fuckers brings a fucking torch to my eyes, and wants me to follow their movements like I'm going to stop looking at Reilly. When I don't move my eyes, Reilly's eyebrows draw down.

"Bray, you have to listen. You need to try, please. Just do what the doctors say. You can do this. Follow the light with your eyes, Bray." Her voice becomes determined, demanding even. I don't want to take my eyes off her, but I also don't want to let her down any more than I have.

I follow the light. As much as it pains me, as much as it causes my head to thump like the hangover of all mother fucking hangovers, I grit down and do it. Just as the doctor's finishing up with the light, the door bursts open and in comes Zac in true Zac form. Demanding, arrogant and fucking assholish. I wouldn't have it any other way. I smile, or at least I think I do. Reilly gasps.

"He smiled. That's good, right?" she asks the doctors. "That's a very good sign, Mrs. Williamson," the doctor says.

There it is again, Mrs. Williamson. If everyone is calling her that, I must have fucking married her. Now, that thought brings a smile to my head. I look at her, ignoring the ruckus that Zac is causing by firing his million questions off to the doctor.

The excitement I see shining in her eyes when I manage to smile up at her gives me a deeper sense of calmness, that everything is going to be okay. That we are going to be okay. I just need to figure out what the fuck is wrong with me and get my body on board with doing what it's supposed to do.

"Why isn't he fucking talking?" Zac growls at the doctor. I turn to watch, trying to focus on what they are talking about. Maybe someone can tell me what the fuck's going on.

"He just woke up from a two-month coma, Mr. Williamson. These things take time. He has shown positive responses to all the tests so far. We need to take him down for another MRI, but everything so far is looking good." The doctor talks directly to Zac, like I'm not in the fucking room.

Reilly must notice my agitated state, though I'm not sure how because I can't fucking move or say anything at the moment. She squeezes my hand and I flick my eyes back to her.

"Bray, do you... do you remember me? Do you know who I am?" she asks, in the softest almost a whisper of a voice.

I catch the croak of her voice; I can feel the fear coming off her, the shake in her hands. Why the fuck would she think I don't remember her? She's not someone anybody would forget.

"Bray, don't speak, okay? Just blink once for yes, twice for no," she says.

I blink once and stare into her eyes. She breathes a sigh of relief. "Oh, thank God. I thought for a moment maybe you forgot just how freaking awesome I am." She smiles down at me.

I want nothing more than to pull her down and kiss her right now, except I can't. I can't do anything. I want a taste of those lips so fucking bad. I stare at them, so fucking plump and delicious. Reilly laughs; it's probably corny as fuck but it's the most beautiful, welcoming sound right now.

She slowly leans down, places her head next to mine and whispers in my ear, "Even though you just woke up, and you might not be able to talk with words, I can still see what you're thinking right now. Those thoughts should not be thought in a room full of doctors, not to mention your brother." She gently places her lips over mine.

I'm in heaven. I just need her to keep those lips on mine. She doesn't; she pulls back after giving me the gentlest kiss, like she's scared she'll break me or something. I want more. I need more. Reilly laughs and shakes her head. "Rye…" I manage to get out a few sounds. I almost just said her whole name. The whole room goes silent, all eyes on me. I'm only looking at one pair of eyes, the ones that belong to the other half of my soul. Her eyes start glistening. Fuck, I've gone and made her fucking cry again.

"Bray, thank fuck. I knew you'd be back with us. I knew you would wake up," Zac says as he leans down to my ear. "Don't you ever fucking scare me like that again, fucker," he not so quietly says. As he straightens back up, he grabs my wrist and squeezes. "I think you actually gave me grey hairs for real this time, Braydon. I'm sending all future hair dye expenses to you because I will not be grey before I'm fifty."

I roll my eyes at him. He's been telling me I'll send him grey since I was sixteen. Luckily for us, we were blessed with good hair genes. My dad was in his mid-fifties when he died, and was only just starting to show signs of greys.

"Za..." I try again to speak. I know what I need to say. My brain is working just fucking fine. Why the fuck isn't my mouth? My throat feels dry, like the Sahara Desert. Water, water would be really bloody good right now.

"Bray, don't try to talk yet. It's okay, man. Trust me, we can wait," Zac says.

"Wa... t... r." I think I manage to get the whole damn word out.

"Water, he needs water... of course he needs water. Why didn't I think of that? He can have water, right?" Reilly lets go of my hand, causing my eyes to search her out. Where is she going? I need her to stay here. I follow her movements; she goes over to the table, where a jug and cup are sitting.

"He can have a couple of small sips; too much and it will make him sick. Very small sips," one of the doctors responds.

I keep my eyes on Reilly, watching her pour a cup of water, place a straw in the cup and bring it back to me. She puts the straw to my lips. I try to follow the doctor's directions and only take a small sip. Just that small bit of water feels like fucking heaven. Reilly takes the cup away before I can get any more. She places it down on the table next to the bed.

"Wha..." I want to ask what happened. She grabs

my hand again, and I feel myself relax into her touch. I turn my eyes to look at Zac, who is watching Reilly with an odd kind of fondness. How long was I fucking asleep for? Did I wake up in the *Twilight Zone*? Zac does not like anybody other than Alyssa and Ella. He barely tolerates me on most days.

I search his eyes for answers. I'm usually pretty good at reading him, just as he is with me. I try to ask again what the fuck happened. "Wha... t?" I get the one word out, eventually. This shit is frustrating as hell. I can hear the monitors' beeping increasing. I can feel myself getting worked up. I'm used to the feeling. I usually relish it, use it as an outlet when I'm training or fighting. Except I can't do either of those right now. I can't fucking move.

"Bray, you were shot. Do you remember?" Zac asks.

I was fucking shot? What cocksucker fucking shot me? A soon to be dead one, when I can get out of this bed. I don't remember getting shot. I can remember flying home from Hawaii. I can remember sleeping at Reilly's house and waking up to her mum's cooked breakfast. After that, I'm drawing a blank.

"N... n... o," I reply.

"You were shot in the abdomen. Nowhere near your fucking head, mind you. Yet you've been in a coma for fifty-nine days. Fifty-nine days, asshole," Zac growls. Fuck, I was out for fifty-nine days? No wonder Reilly was sobbing when I came to. Has she been waiting here that whole time? Why didn't someone look after her? Help her?

The thought of her sitting by my bed, day in and day out, both pisses me off and makes me happy as fuck that she's mine. She's the most loyal girl you'll ever meet, and she's fucking mine.

# CHAPTER TWENTY-THREE

REILLY

E'S COMING HOME TODAY. I actually get to take Bray home today. I feel like I've been waiting for this day to arrive forever. Yet, for Bray, I'd probably wait the rest of my life. If I had to spend my life living in a hospital to be with him, then so be it, I'd do it. I can't be without him. That fact has been made abhorrently clear.

I came so close to losing him. I've never been one to take my loved ones for granted. I already knew they could be taken away in the blink of an eye. It's the very reason I pushed Bray away so much at first, why I didn't want to get involved with him. I knew that if I let myself love him, then I'd really freaking love him. Which also meant I'd be left in pieces when I lost him.

The last six weeks have been gruelling, gut-wrench-ing, an emotional rollercoaster. Bray has undergone intense physical therapy to be able to relearn every-thing. It was tough, watching him push himself day after day to do the most basic of tasks like walking, dressing, eating. But it's all paid off. He is now able to walk unassisted; it's still at a slower pace and at times unsteady, but he is walking. His speech came back to normal after two weeks.

The first full sentence he uttered was to tell me he loved me. After I bawled my eyes out, because I honestly never thought I'd hear those words again, I told him just how much I loved his ass and asked him to marry me. I did not get the reaction I would have hoped for.

*"I love you," Bray said—the full sentence—no stops, pauses or breaks. He just told me he loved me in one fell swoop. I can feel the tears well in my eyes. I don't even try to stop them, letting them fall. Bray telling me he loves me is something I thought I'd never hear again.*

*Once I compose myself again, I tell him, "I love you so much, it hurts. I love you more than I thought I could love anyone. You complete me, Bray. I always thought Holly was my other half, but it seems I have another, and that's you. You are the other half of my soul. As soon as we get out of here, I want you to fly me away and marry me." Bray's eyebrows draw in, his eyes shining with unshed tears. "I... already." He points between us both. "Married?" he questions. As I'm trying to decipher, he points to me and says, "Mrs."*

*Then he pauses again before he gets the words out. "Call you Mrs.," he says while pointing to the door.*

*He thinks we are already married because all the doctors and nurses refer to me as Mrs. Williamson. Huh, I never thought to correct any of them. I liked being called Mrs. Williamson, so I let it continue so long that I forgot why it started in the first place.*

*"Wait, you think we're already married? Do you remember getting married, Braydon?" I wait for his answer. To which, he shakes his head no.*

*"No, you know why, because we haven't. Trust me, the day you marry me, you are not going to forget. I'm a damn catch!" I laugh.*

*Bray's eyebrows raise in question. I've gotten really good at reading his gestures and figuring out what he needs or wants over the last two weeks. Right now, he wants more information.*

*"Right. When you were first brought in, the doctor was questioning how I was your family. Zac was there and, without flinching, he told him I was your wife. I just let the little lie continue all this time."*

*I watch as Bray's face lights up; his smile is a welcoming sight that I want to spend the rest of my life receiving.*

Over the next four weeks, as Bray's speech improved, we spent nights planning out our life together. We talked endlessly about what we wanted. Bray wanted eight kids. I vetoed that straight away and said maybe two, definitely no more than three. His reply was, "Babe, junior's boys are champions; they're going to impregnate you quicker than you can blink. They're just going to swim right on up and pop those eggs of yours."

I didn't bother to argue, but in my head, I was reminding myself to make a doctor's appointment for birth control, ASAP. I'd let mine lapse over the last few months. It's not like junior was getting anywhere near my eggs, not that Bray didn't try to persuade me. The number of times he told me to lock the door and *climb on*—yeah, it didn't take long for him to be able to say those words—I denied him. There was no way I was doing anything to jeopardise his recovery. The most he got, because I kind of felt bad for junior, was my hand and mouth. Although, I won't lie, it was different without feeling the metal of his Prince Albert. The doctors removed it the day he got brought in.

I told him how much I was going to miss that thing; he promised he was making an appointment with the piercer to get it back. I silently thanked the gods. Because that tiny bit of metal gives an unbelievable amount of pleasure.

Pleasure like I've never felt before it. Not that Bray's junior isn't impressive without it, because it is.

I'm watching Bray as he dresses. We're waiting on Zac to come and pick us up. Both of us cannot wait to get out of here and go home. I haven't told Bray, I didn't even ask, I just took the liberty and moved myself into his house. I figured he asked me to move in with him enough times before the incident, the offer would still stand.

I had Holly arrange for my things to be moved. My mum cried. She's been amazing throughout this process, spending many hours just sitting in the hospital with us. When Bray woke up, she made sure to visit every other day with baked treats for him. I wasn't allowed to eat any of them.

It pains me to watch how much effort it's taking him to get dressed by himself, to do a simple thing like pull his sweats up and put a shirt over his head. I want to help him, I'm itching to help him, but he's determined to do it all himself. The fact that he's a fighter has never been clearer than it has been watching him through his recovery. He was able to push through pain, frustration and fatigue like I've never seen before.

I admire his grit and determination. I admire how much he fought to be able to achieve the simple things most take for granted. He never gave up; he pushed his body beyond limits that even the doctors were amazed at the speed of his physical recovery. I won't lie, as he stands before me in a pair of grey sweats, no shirt, no shoes, I'm kind of enjoying the slowness of that shirt being pulled on.

My eyes travel up and down his body. He's lost a fair bit of his muscle mass, but he's still toned and defined as hell. The things I want to do to that body. I lick my dry lips recalling the things I have done to, and with, that body. I'm lost in my thoughts until Bray breaks my daydream, my very enjoyable daydream.

"Babe, unless you want me to bend you over this bed and fuck you senseless right now, you need to stop looking at me like you've just seen a tall glass of water in the desert." He finishes his comment with that smirk, the one he knows makes my damn panties wet, just at the sight of it.

I look up at the clock, like I'm actually considering his offer. As much as I want to, there is no way that's happening here. In this hospital room.

"As appealing as that offer is, your brother should be here any minute." I shrug in a too bad kind of motion.

"I'll lock the door and he can fucking wait," Bray offers, just as said brother walks through the door.

"Who can wait? You guys ready to blow this place or what?" he asks.

"I'm ready, so ready," I tell him, as I get up and greet him with a hug. Yep, apparently that happens now. Zac and I, friends? Who would have thought? "Thank you for picking us up."

"I'm doing it for you; that asshole made us wait fifty-nine fucking days. It would only be fair if we made him wait on a ride home."

Zac reminds Bray as often as he can that he slept for fifty-nine days. Tortured us for fifty-nine days. Not that he had any control over it, Zac knows that, but I've learnt that's how they communicate with each other.

"You know, I'm still not sure if I'm on board with this newfound friendship with you two. It's not fair to gang up on the injured. Whatever happened to rooting for the underdog?" Bray says.

"Deal with it. Reilly is my new sister, so if you fuck up again and I have to watch her heart break, again, I'm gonna kick your fucking ass," Zac says, with a very serious tone in his voice.

"I'd let you kick my ass. But, I'm not planning on fucking up again. We're getting married, we're having eight babies and we are going to grow old and grey together." Bray walks up and wraps his arm around me.

"Two. Two babies," I correct him.

"So I keep hearing." Zac rolls his eyes. It's true, Bray mentions the fact that we're getting married and having babies as often as he can drop it in conversation.

He even has all the nurses swooning over him. Which brings me back to the shirt. There is no way in hell, he's walking out there with only a pair of grey sweats on. I'd end up having to claw some eyes out for sure.

I walk over to the bed where he left his shirt and pick it up. I don't bother handing it to him. I pull it over his head and let him do the rest. Once he has his shirt on, it's no better. He still looks like sex on legs. Damn it, I really need to get laid. Soon. As I'm looking him up and down, I can feel myself getting more and more turned on.

"Reilly," Bray growls, snapping me from my dirty thoughts, again. He really needs to stop interrupting my thought process.

"Okay, if you two are finished eye-fucking each other, let's get out of here." Zac picks up the two bags by the door and leaves the room.

I take hold of Bray's hand and walk out with him. Walk out of this dreary, cold place and into our future. He once made me a promise that he would always fight for us, because we were worth fighting for. He kept that promise. He has fought day in and day out to get back to who he once was, to be able to give us the future we both so desperately want and dream of.

# EPILOGUE

*Bray*

*Six months later*

*I*'M speechless when Reilly comes out of the bathroom in a white lace corset, white lace thong and thigh-high stockings. She's fucking perfection standing there, leaning against the door frame while waiting for me to say something, to give her instruction. I'm not finished admiring the view of my wife though, so she can wait a little longer.

My wife, that goddess right there is my fucking wife. I want to run up to the top of this Vegas high-rise and scream it out for all to hear. I, Bray Williamson, put a ring on it and locked it down.

It's been a tough six months. My recovery seems to have taken its time. Although the doctors say I made great progress and recovered quicker than anyone they've seen, I feel like it's taken longer than necessary. The hardest part of this mess is not being able to fight. I tried to get everyone on board with me entering the ring again. I had coach at the house every other day going through routines and training.

Every doctor has advised against it, but they're doctors; they're meant to advise against shit like that. The thing that made me wake up, made me realise that there is much more to life than fighting, was Reilly. The look of utter shock and horror that would cross her face whenever I mentioned going back in the cage.

She was never all for me fighting before, but she never looked like I killed her cat while discussing it before either.

When I asked her about why she looked so terrified her reply was, "I spent two months sitting by your bedside waiting for you to wake up. I spent two months praying to a god I wasn't even sure existed anymore. I spent two months thinking I had lost the best thing to ever happen to me. I don't ever want to experience that kind of pain again. I won't stop you. I won't ask you not to fight, that has to be completely your own decision. Whatever you decide, I'll still be your biggest cheerleader."

I was just as speechless then as I am now. After replaying her words through my head for two weeks, I decided not to go back in the cage. I thought I'd feel a loss at the thought of never fighting again. What I felt was a weight lifted. I still get antsy, my body itching with energy that needs to be moving at times. When this happens, I either seek out Reilly to expel energy together, or I hit the gym and give myself a gruelling workout.

In the last six months, I've managed to regain all the muscle loss that happened after the shooting. It's been a long slow process, but I finally feel like my old self. It was fucking torture those first few months, not being able to get up and walk, do normal mundane everyday things like button up my own fucking clothes. If it wasn't for Reilly and Zac constantly being by my side throughout the recovery, I probably would have gone mad or given up completely.

"*Ahh,* Bray, are you just going to sit there staring all night?" Reilly's voice snaps me out of my own head.

"Well, when the views this good, why the hell not?" I question her.

"For one, it's our wedding night, and you only get one shot at making a memorable wedding night. Two, these shoes, as hot as they look, really are not comfortable and I can't stand here all night." She stomps one of those ridiculously high stilettos on the floor.

I don't make an effort to move. I stay seated on the edge of the bed. I started stripping my clothes off while Reilly was in the bathroom. I got down to just my trousers when she opened the door and I had to sit my ass down before I fell at her feet. She took the breath right out of me.

"Your feet hurt, babe?" I ask, watching as she nods her head.

"What kind of husband would I be if I let my wife get sore feet on our first night of being married? Not a very good one, and I plan to be the best husband who ever existed. Not sure if you noticed, but I'm fucking great husband material. It's like you won the lottery of husbands when you said *I do* tonight."

Reilly laughs. "I want to disagree and bust that ego of yours a little, but we don't lie to each other, so I won't disagree. I did win the lottery of husbands."

As I take her in, I recall the moment she said I do, earlier tonight in a Vegas chapel. We did end up running off to Vegas to get married. We did however let our family tag along. We also switched things up. I wasn't as stupid as Zac. I knew Reilly didn't have her dad to walk her down the aisle. When I questioned her about what she wanted to do, because I was not about to let her walk down that aisle alone, she got teary and told me that nobody could replace her dad's spot.

She then decided that we would walk down together, that it was our wedding and we could make the rules. The idea of walking down the aisle together as equals, as partners, was fucking brilliant. My girl is a fucking genius. So that's what we did—we met at the end of the aisle and walked down hand in hand. After I spent a good five minutes trying to convince her to sneak off to a closet with me first.

She told me to wait, some crap about delayed gratification. So now I'm going to make her wait. First, I need to deal with her aching feet, because there is no way she's removing those shoes until after they've spent hours digging into my back.

"Kneel," I tell her, my voice leaving no room for argument. "Right where you are now, kneel."

Reilly glares at me; this is not what she wanted. Too bad she's not the one running this show. After a minute of glaring, she relents. Following my instruction, she kneels, sitting back on her heels. I don't miss the slight shiver that runs through her body as she does this.

"Put your hands on your knees."

I wait for her to follow the instruction. Silently, she places her hands on her knees, palms down.

"Pull your legs apart, as far as they go. I want to see that pretty pussy I own."

Reilly licks her lips as she slowly spreads her legs apart. She's so responsive to being ordered around in the bedroom. Try to tell her to do something outside of the bedroom and I get a completely different reaction. Her tiny thong does nothing to cover her. It's basically see- through with how wet it is.

Inhaling, I can smell her arousal from here. I can see her pussy dripping for me; it's like a beacon, a siren calling for me to pet it. And pet it, I plan to. Tilting my head to the side, I look her over. I still can't believe that she's mine. I need to keep this scene locked away in my memories. I don't ever want to forget this moment.

"I hope you weren't counting on a night of slow passionate love making, babe, because I plan to fuck you so hard you won't be able to walk straight tomorrow."

"Well, what are you waiting for?"

"Delayed gratification, babe. Good things come to those who wait." I replay her own words back to her.

Reilly growls at me. "Bray, do not make me wait, please."

Fuck, she uses that please like a fucking weapon. She knows I can never deny her anything when she uses that please. Getting up off the bed, I walk over to her slowly, and a small smirk crosses her face. She thinks she's won. Little does she know, I'm planning on toying with her as long as I possibly can. I don't ever want this night to end.

Grabbing her with my hand around her throat, I tip her head back. Bringing my face down to hers, I gently brush my lips along hers as I make my way to her ear. While trailing the fingers of my other hand along the top of her breast, I whisper, "I hope you're comfortable, babe. I'm not planning to rush through my dessert tonight. I'm going to take my time, relish in the sweetness that I know is waiting for me. I'm going to lap up the weeping juices like it's my last meal and savour it."

Reilly moans; she goes to close her legs. I know she's dying to get some friction to her core. Squeezing tighter on her neck, I growl at her, "Don't you dare close those fucking legs, Reilly."

With a grunt, she spreads them back open. With my hand still around her throat, I hold her still as my lips attack her neck before making their way down to the tops of her breasts. This corset is in my fucking way. I can't get to those delicious pink nipples I want so bad. I stand and make my way over to the dining table and pick up a steak knife.

Reilly doesn't even flinch when I bring the knife back, running the tip of it along the skin of her neck and breast. She really fucking trusts me a lot. Pulling the fabric of the corset away from her skin, so I don't fucking cut her, I slice right down the middle—her breasts bouncing as they're freed from their confines.

I don't waste time getting my mouth and hands on those pink nipples, positioning myself between her legs to prevent her from being able to close them. I take my time sucking and biting on each nipple. Reilly is a writhing mess by the time I come up for air. Her moans fill the room, as she attempts to push me away one minute, only to pull me closer the next, with the hold she has on my head while pulling at my hair.

I kiss my way down her stomach, before twisting and laying my head on the ground between her spread legs. Reaching up, I grab her hips and lift her, positioning her just where I want her, with her pussy right above my face. Ripping the tiny piece of lace that attempts to cover her, I slowly glide my tongue along her slit, from top to bottom.

She falls forward the moment my tongue connects with her clit, her hands landing on the tops of my thighs. It doesn't take her long before those same hands are travelling up and undoing my pants and releasing junior.

As she slowly strokes her hand up and down my cock, I continue my slow attack on her pussy.

The moment her tongue licks the slit in my tip, twirling around my piercing, I almost lose control. Fuck that feels good. I'm not about to lose out in the first round. Sliding my tongue right up to her puckered hole, I lick and twirl around it. This is a move I know drives her insane. She starts bucking against my face, attempting to grind down on me, and I have to hold her hips to keep her still. No doubt, she will be left with my fingerprints all over those hips tomorrow.

I slowly slide two fingers in and out of her pussy while licking around her back hole. She's so fucking close that she's all but forgotten about junior while her attempts to stay focused on her task are weak. I fucking love seeing her fall apart and to be the one, the only one, making her see the fucking stars.

Picking up the speed, I thrust my fingers in harder and harder, while flattening my tongue out on her hole. She grinds down on me, screaming my name as she comes undone before falling flat on top of me. After a few minutes, Reilly slides off me and onto the floor.

Deciding I've given her enough recovery time, I stand, pick her up, and throw her down on the bed. She squeals as she lands in the middle of the bed. I strip out of my pants before crawling up her body. She looks so fucking perfect, her red hair sprawled out above her like a halo. Her pale skin is glistening with goose-bumps. As I look down at her, I send a little prayer up, thanking God that this woman is mine.

"I fucking love you so damn much, Reilly Williamson." I look into her eyes and I can see the pure love she has for me too.

"I love you more than you'll ever know, Bray. More than words can describe." She reaches up, wrapping her hands above my neck and pulling my lips down to connect with hers. I know I wanted to fuck her until she couldn't walk tomorrow. Plans change though, right now all I want to do is love her the way she deserves to be loved.

That's how we spend the rest of our first night of being husband and wife, making sweet, tender love, over and over again. Our bodies and souls fused together as one, and I wouldn't have it any other fucking way.

*Reilly*

*Two years later*

"Aunty Rye Rye!" Ashton, the little chubby two and a half year old runs up to me, arms stretched high. Just as I'm about to attempt to bend down to him, Bray swoops in, lifting him up in his arms.

"Ash, my man. You know Aunty Rye Rye can't pick you up," he says while ruffling Ashton's hair.

"Babies," Ashton says, pointing at my obvious, expanding stomach that is now the size of a house. I guess in a way it is a home.

"Yeah, mate, Aunty Rye Rye has uncle Bray's babies in there," Bray confirms. I roll my eyes at him.

He loves to drop that line as often as he can. He knocked me up, not once, but twice in the one go. Yep, I'm pregnant with twins, and he's taking all the credit for them being twins. Never mind the fact that I am a twin, and that the genetics for twins comes from me, not him.

"Yes, Ash, it is all Uncle Bray's fault that I have babies in my tummy making it so big," I tell him, kissing his cheek.

"Big babies," Ash says, rubbing my belly while I glare at Bray.

"See, even our two-year-old nephew agrees that I'm fat." I'm so grumpy; pregnancy has not been my friend and I still have three months to go.

"Babe, you are not fat. You are fucking gorgeous, glowing even," Bray says as he leans in and kisses me on my forehead. That's his move to calm me, and it works every damn time.

"Ash, mate, clearly your dad has not taught you very well yet. You don't tell the girls they have big tummies; you can tell them they have big boo—" He's cut off by Alyssa's scream.

"Do not think about finishing that sentence, Braydon. I will knock you down. I've done it once. I can do it again," she yells across the room.

Zac walks up and plucks Ash from Bray's arms, then slaps him across the back of the head. "You fucking idiot, do not teach my son your man-whoring ways."

Bray stumbles back, hand over heart. "*Ahh*, bro, that hurts. Besides, who do you think I learnt it from, *huh*? I'll tell you, I learnt it from watching—"

Bray's sentence dies off with the icy glare that Zac throws his way. I swear even after three years, that guy can still scare me with that glare.

"Watching Jersey Shore," Bray finishes, saving himself from another slap to the head.

"You know those two babies you impregnated your wife with?" Zac asks.

"Yep, know them well," Bray answers with a huge smile across his face.

Zac smirks, nods his head towards my belly and says, "They're both girls, bro. Those babies are girls, and with any luck, they're going to look like their mother."

The smile from Bray's face completely vanishes. He goes a bit pale before he recovers. "Shut up, they are going to be nuns. Reilly, we're joining a fucking church tomorrow."

Alyssa, Sarah, Holly and I all burst into laughter standing in the middle of my kitchen. I stop laughing just as quickly as I start. "Sorry, gotta pee," I say, dashing out of the room. Over my shoulder I yell, "But thanks for calling me hot, Zac!"

"Not what I said," he calls back.

I finish in the bathroom, walk back out and see everyone has made their way out to the deck—Zac, Bray and Dean all surrounding the BBQ while the girls sit on the lounge sipping glasses of wine. Man, I miss wine.

I stop and admire the scene. Little Ashton is playing

out on the grass. Bray had a play gym installed for him the day after he was born, claiming that it was part of his best uncle duties. It's taken two years, but Ashton is just now big enough to play on it, under the ever-watchful eye of Zac—his eyes constantly wandering between Ashton and Alyssa. I can't believe that this is my family now.

The ringing doorbell pulls me away from the scene. I pull it open to my mum, holding a tray of baked goods. Rolling my eyes at her, I open the door to let her in. It's become her and Bray's thing; whenever she visits, she brings him baked goods, and no one else is ever allowed to eat them.

"Hey, mum." I kiss her cheek.

"How're you feeling, sweetie? How are my grandbabies in there? Is your mummy looking after you?" she talks to my stomach.

"Your grandbabies want one of those chocolate brownies," I say, reaching for the tray, only to have her pull it away.

"Don't even think about it, Reilly. You know these are for Bray."

I give up, nothing works on her. If it was my dad, I'd be able to wrangle those brownies. But not mum, she doesn't fall for any of my tricks.

"Everyone's out back," I say, walking her through the house. I used to think of this house as overly huge with a lot of wasted space, but now that the twins are coming, I'm thankful that we have so much room. Bray said when he bought it, he wanted to fill it with a football team of children; it just took him a while to find his co-coach.

He's dreaming if he thinks I'm letting myself get knocked up again. As much as I'm looking forward to these little girls coming into the world, pregnancy is not for the faint-hearted. I blame Alyssa; she made it look easy.

As soon as my mother is out on the deck, Bray has her engulfed in a hug. "Lynne, I'm so glad you're here. Maybe you can help me convince your daughter that we should join a church."

I glare at Bray. Holly throws something—I think it's a piece of bread. It hits his head but bounces right off.

"We are not joining a church, Bray," I say, falling into a seat next to Holly.

"Well, I think it's a lovely idea," my mother says—of course she does. Bray just asked an Irish Catholic mother if we should go to church.

"Bray, why don't you tell my mum why it is exactly, that you want to join the church." I smirk at him.

Holly high-fives me. She knows once my mum hears the nonsense, she will switch to our team.

"So our babies, your granddaughters, can become nuns," Bray says so seriously; to which, my mum laughs her ass off.

"Oh, hunny, Bray. I'm sorry, but if those babies turn out anything like their mother, you're going to be chasing boys away from the age of ten." She then scrunches her face up and adds, "Actually, if I recall, the first time Reilly kissed a boy, she was three. It was at a play group and she was adamant that the little boy was her boyfriend. No matter how much her dad told her she wasn't allowed to have boyfriends."

Bray looks over at me in shock. I just shrug at him. I can't help it if I appreciated boys from a young age. He then turns to look out at the yard and calls out to Ash.

"Hey, Ash." He waits for Ash to turn around.

"You and I are going to start training. I'm teaching you how to kick ass, mate," Bray declares, walking up to him and picking him up.

Everyone else is laughing, but the problem is Bray's not kidding. He seriously is going to start teaching Ash how to fight. As he reaches the top of the deck again, Zac is quick to pinch Ash out of Bray's hands.

"*Aw*, come on, man. He needs to learn how to protect his little cousins." Bray then looks at Alyssa.

"You..." He points to her. "You need to start pumping out some more boys. We're gonna need an army." Alyssa looks horrified.

"Me? Why me? You have a perfectly young and fertile sister you know, goes by the name of Ella," Alyssa informs him.

Both Zac and Bray groan and screw up their noses. "No," they say at the same time.

"Fuck no," Bray says again, shaking his head and adding extra emphasis to the no.

I expected their reaction, but what makes me

curious is Dean's reaction. He goes still, looking back and forward between the two brothers. They're in front of him so they can't see him, or his reaction.

"You know, she's not a baby anymore. It's bound to happen," he says.

Both brothers turn and glare at him. Bray, who happens to know just how Ella feels about Dean, raises his eyebrows.

"Oh, and just who do you think it's going to happen with?" he asks, then furthers his point, trying to elicit a reaction from Dean. "You think Ella's in her apartment now, busy with some university jock she met last night?"

Dean's face goes blank. Got to give it to the guy, he has one hell of a poker face when he needs it. I notice his hands clench and unclench though. He does not like that thought at all. I can't wait to see how this plays out in the future. That man is in love, stupid for denying it, but in love he is.

"She is studying. I had a call from her earlier. She's alone in her apartment, idiot," Zac says to Bray.

"I know that. I spoke to her an hour ago," Bray confirms. It amazes me how much these two can't let go of their baby sister. It's also endearing to know that my girls are going to experience that same unconditional love.

Bray is going to be the best father. He excelled at being the best boyfriend, he excelled at being the best husband and I know he will be the best father.

"Bray, can you help me up?" I hold out my hands to him.

I can fully get up on my own, sort of; I just want an excuse to touch him and pull him away from everyone else. He walks over and pulls me up, not letting go of my hands until he knows I have even footing. I grab his hand and pull him inside.

"I need you to, *ahh*, help me reach something in the kitchen," I say maybe a bit too loudly.

Once inside, I pull his mouth down to mine. I'm so hungry for him. I thought I was horny a lot before, but that has nothing on these bloody pregnancy hormones. I moan into his mouth as he takes over the kiss.

We eventually pull apart, breathing heavier than we were before. "You good?" he asks while pushing my hair out of my face.

"I'm good. I just really, really love you." This is nothing new to him. I tell him multiple times a day how much I love and appreciate him.

"I really fucking love you too," he replies.

I get lost for a moment in those green orbs of his. I thank God that he was able to bulldoze those walls of mine down. I thank God every day that our souls are fused together as one.

Want more?
Get the Bonus Scene here: Zac & Alyssa - The Wedding

# ACKNOWLEDGMENTS

I am thankful first to you, the reader, the one for whom this story was written. And I hope that you enjoyed the characters and the emotional rollercoaster that is Bray and Reilly's relationship.

For months, Bray and Reilly lived within me, urging me to get their story told. Being able to translate my random thoughts and daydreams into a real-life written story is a dream come true to me. Having people read and enjoy my story is icing on the cake, so thank you, readers!!!

I am thankful to my family. My wonderful husband; whose support and endless encouragement never fails. Nate, I could not have accomplished this without you.

I am thankful for my Sister, Lynne-Maree. Thank you for the endless conversations I made you listen to about Bray and Reilly as they took over my life.

Thank you, Reilly, my very real best friend Reilly. Thank you for falling in love and claiming Bray as your very first book boyfriend!

Thank you, thank you, thank you to Shannan, my

very wonderful and patient editor. Thank you for helping me

along the journey of publishing this book baby with me. Thank you for your endless positive reinforcements and encouragements along the way. Thank you for embracing the characters, investing in their story just as much as I did. I could not have gotten to this point without you.

My beta readers: Natasha, Heather, Janel and Allie. Thank you. You girls are truly amazing. I am forever humbled that you once took a chance on this little unknown author from Australia and stuck around for book two. Thank you for all of the time and effort you put into reading and providing insightful feedback for *Fused With Him*.

The Kylie Kent Street Team, what can I say? I would literally be nowhere if it weren't for you. I often get asked by other authors how I managed to form my street team. My answer is always the same: one hundred percent pure luck, and I'm not ever giving them back!! I believe I have the BEST street team in the business. Not only do you all ARC read for me, but you all read, promote and share whatever I put in front of you so enthusiastically and with genuine interest and excitement. I freaking love you guys!

I want to thank the guy I just happened to stumble across on TikTok. For months, I searched high and low for the perfect cover model to represent Bray. I had a very particular image in my head of Bray (as I'm sure you all do). I could not find him anywhere. And I looked under every nook and cranny. I was really starting to believe that I created the character that didn't really exist.

Except he did; I knew he was out there somewhere. After casually scrolling through TikTok, while procrastinating from writing, I found this guy. At first, I thought my eyes were seeing things. I actually thought I had gone and lost my mind—finally—because right there on my "for you" page was Bray. The real-life freaking Bray, dancing and strutting his stuff. I possibly then spent the next hour, or two (who's to know) stalking this guy's TikTok and Instagram account. He ticked off all the boxes: abs, arms, tattoos, dark hair, great eyes and a smile that's going to melt your panties right off.

I knew I needed this guy on my cover and I also knew there was no way I was going to be able to message him and ask him myself. So, I sent my trusty friend Tash on the job. Long story short, he agreed to do the cover shot—not only agreed to do it, but was excited and enthusiastic to be doing it. I could not have asked for a better cover model to be Bray. So, thank you, Blaze Almon, for agreeing to let romance readers everywhere picture you as their real-life Braydon Williamson. I cannot wait to be able to see you on the cover of many, many more romance novels.

Last but not least, thank you to all of the awesome and inspiring authors and readers I have met through social media over the course of this process. Thank you for welcoming a newbie like me into your author communities and taking the time to answer questions and encourage me along my journey.

Printed in Great Britain
by Amazon